Mates, Mysteries and Pretty Weird Weirdness

"Well, tomorrow … Sam's coming up to Crouch End to see me!" Kyra beamed.

"Brilliant!" I smiled, genuinely pleased for her. "Are you excited?"

"Yeah, but a bit … y'know … nervous, too," she surprised me by saying. "Which is why I want you to come too, Ally."

"What?" I squeaked at Kyra, not sure I'd heard right.

"I just thought it I wouldn't be so … y'know … awkward, if you were there, Ally. Oh, and another thing," she grinned sheepishly from the other side of the garden gate. "Can you bring Billy along? Just so Sam doesn't feel outnumbered by girls? 'Cause I thought if you pretended Billy was your boyfriend then…"

Whoah – maybe I was intrigued enough to meet the mighty Sam, and maybe friends are expected to do each other favours, but pretending Billy was my boyfriend? Wasn't that way beyond the call of duty…?

To find out more about Karen McCombie,
visit her website www.karenmccombie.com

KaReN McCoMbie

MaTeS,
MYSTERIES aNd
PReTTY WeiRd
WeiRdNeSS

SCHOLASTIC

for freddie, the original
gnome-shifting culprit...

First published in the UK in 2002 by Scholastic Children's Books
An imprint of Scholastic Ltd
Euston House, 24 Eversholt Street
London, NW1 1DB, UK
Registered office: Westfield Road, Southam, Warwickshire, CV47 0RA
SCHOLASTIC and associated logos are trademarks and or registered
trademarks of Scholastic Inc.

This edition published by Scholastic Ltd, 2007

Text copyright © Karen McCombie, 2002
The right of Karen McCombie to be identified as the author of this work has
been asserted by her.

Cover illustration copyright © Spike Gerrell, 2002

10 digit ISBN 0 439 94286 1
13 digit ISBN 978 0439 94286 7

British Library Cataloguing-in-Publication Data.
A CIP catalogue record for this book is available from the British Library

Printed in the UK by CPI Bookmarque, Croydon, CR0 4TD
Papers used by Scholastic Children's Books are made from wood grown in
sustainable forests.

3 5 7 9 10 8 6 4 2

www.scholastic.co.uk/zone

Contents

PROLOGUE

Dear Mum,

I don't mean to worry you, but Rowan's brain seems to have melted in the heat. (Will anyone notice the difference?)

It's just that it's so baking hot today that she came up with an interesting way of keeping cool – making ice-cubes. But not normal H_2O ice-cubes of course – that would be *way* too simple for Rowan. She's currently sitting on a deckchair in the garden sucking furiously on *custard* ice-cubes, while huffing at me and Tor for refusing to try one and not appreciating her efforts. I'm sorry, but I'd rather splash my face with water out of the dogs' bowl* to keep cool than suck frozen custard.

Speaking of dogs, we all fell in love with that cute golden retriever in the background of the photo that came with your latest letter (all the way from Dallas, Texas!) this morning. Did you notice it? It looked like a wet mop, coming soaking out of the sea. If you didn't notice it then you sure must have *felt* it from the way it was spin-drying itself about five centimetres behind you. But you know something? There were two kind of weird things about your photo and letter: 1) that dog looked practically identical to one that was destroying a sandcastle in the background of a photo you sent from Hawaii a couple of months ago; and 2) when I went upstairs to put a pin on the map to point out where you were, I realized that there aren't any beaches near Dallas, *or* near Texas (by about a zillion kilometres). Ho hum...

Still, two more bits of weirdness hardly matter at the moment – my world has been one gigantic dollop of pretty weird weirdness lately. I'd better tell you all. So, are you sitting comfortably, Mum, wherever you are? Then I'll begin (over the page)...
Love you lots,
Ally
(your Love Child No. 3)

* I caught Tor doing that a few minutes ago – splashing his face with water out of the dogs' bowl, I mean. After running around the lawn, demented, for the last hour, Tor, Rolf and Winslet are now all collapsed in the shade of the garden shed in a panting, overheated tangle of boy and dogs. Honestly, that kid is one step away from barking and sniffing lamp-posts...

Chapter 1

WEIRD BUT KIND OF WONDERFUL

"Ouch!" I mumbled under my breath, as a vicious cactus prickled my bare leg. I leapt back out of its spiny way and immediately felt a disgusting squishing sensation under my elbow. Slowly I lifted my arm to inspect the damage, and saw a dollop of red *ooze* drip from my elbow and land with a splat on my denim cut-offs.

Understandably, I guessed that a chunk of my skin had somehow been gouged away and leapt forward in shock, only to find myself being smothered – by a huge pair of white pants.

And then I woke up.

No, I didn't – I just suddenly remembered that you can't daydream on Kellie's balcony, you really need to be on your guard at all times. Other tenants in the building might keep the odd pot plant perched out here in the fresh air, or hang out a few pairs of socks to dry in the breeze. Kellie's mother, however, has turned their shoebox-sized balcony into a cross between the Hanging Gardens of Babylon and a laundrette.

Bored of waiting for Salma to turn up so we could all get out in the sunshine this Friday afternoon, I'd ambled out here, found myself gawping at the badly sunburnt bald spot of the guy on the pavement down below (yeah, well, the *main* view you get from the balcony of Kellie's third-floor flat is of … the three-storey block of flats right across the street) and lost my concentration for a second. That's when I'd leant a little too close to the cactus collection, backed into the tomato plant (squish) and had a close encounter of the knicker kind with Mrs Vincent's pegged-up smalls. (Make that "bigs"…)

"Salma's here!" Jen stuck her head out of the metal-framed door. "You coming in, Ally?"

"Course!" I nodded, hoping she didn't catch the fact that I'd been on the verge of wiping tomato gloop off my elbow with the nearest available piece of material – i.e. Kellie's mum's gigantic undies…

"Here," I heard her say as I stepped into the shade of the living room and waited for my eyes to adjust from the blinding brightness outside.

"Thanks," I muttered, taking a tissue from the box Jen was holding out to me and wiping my soggy arm. (Urgh – she *had* spotted me!)

"Great!" I heard Kellie say (even if I couldn't quite focus on her), as she walked back into the room with Salma. "Now that everyone's here, *wait* till I show you what *I* got today!"

Half a second of rapid blinking and I was able to glance around and confirm that the "everyone" that Kellie was talking to included me, Chloe, Salma and Jen. It didn't include Sandie – who was away for a few days with her parents visiting assorted relatives; or Kyra – who was out shopping with her mum (i.e. right this second in some store in Oxford Street there would be *lots* of arguing and wheedling going on).

"What is it?" I asked Kellie, intrigued. But I was less intrigued by whatever was in the bottom of Kellie's bag than in her general furtiveness. That gagging-to-tell-you look on her face was one thing, but the way she kept checking over her shoulders as she rummaged in her rucksack made me wonder if she had a top-secret government file in there on the abolition of lipgloss or homework or something and was expecting MI5 to burst into her flat any second now and drag her away screaming to a cell.

"Look!" grinned Kellie, holding up a book for us all to examine while she took another surreptitious glance over her shoulder.

"Wow!" gasped Chloe, studying the dog-eared

book cover. "*The Cacti Grower's Guide*! That's *fascinating*, Kellie!"

Kellie frowned at Chloe's sarcasm and flipped the book around, checking the cover for herself.

"Oh. I got that one for my mum," she mumbled, chucking it to one side and diving her hand back inside the bag. "I went to this car-boot sale with my cousin Letitia this morning and picked up some stuff dead cheap, like ... *this*!"

With a grand flourish, she held up a book for our inspection.

"*The Little Book of Lovey-Dovey Spells*," I said out loud, in case all my friends had lost the ability to read during the summer holidays.

"Ooh! *Cool!* Let's have a look at that!" gasped Chloe, turning from sarky to shrieky with excitement in the space of two seconds.

"It was only 50p, but it's full of these *excellent* spells for finding true love," Kellie explained, as Chloe yanked the book out of her hands and began flicking through the pages – Salma and Jen crowding in on her on either side of the sofa for a nosey. With no room to join them, I scrambled around the back and leant my (tomato-free) elbows on the cushioned ledge of the sofa back.

"Here!" Chloe surprised me by saying, snapping the book shut and passing it over her head and into my hands. "*You* pick one out, Ally, and read it in that funny voice you do!"

"Yeah – go on, Al!" Salma turned and grinned up at me.

Oh. I hadn't realized that I *did* a "funny" voice. But I didn't mind having a go. Quickly, I flicked through the pages of weird but kind of wonderful spells and settled on one with a stupid name (well, I would, wouldn't I?).

"OK – here we go," I began, straightening up and getting myself ready to launch into a suitably spooksome delivery. "'The Totally, Utterly Charming Charm'."

"Ooh! I'm getting goosebumps already!"

"Shut up, Kel!" Salma grinned down at Kellie, all curled up on the floor, her arms gripping her knees close to her chest. "Let Ally get on with it!"

"'For best results,'" I got on with it, "'do this spell as the clock strikes midnight!'"

"Not fair!" whined Jen. "I can *never* stay awake till then, even when I try!"

"Yeah, of course," Chloe narrowed her green eyes at Jen, "you have to be tucked up in your jim-jams by eight so your mummy can read you a bedtime story!"

I gave a loud cough before war broke out, just to remind the girls what we were supposed to be doing.

"Ignore them, Al! *I* want to hear!" Salma encouraged me.

"Anyway, it says here that you need a seashell, a pinch of nutmeg, a hair from your head—"

"Well, where *else* would it be from?" Chloe interrupted, with a rude snigger.

"Ally! You've stopped doing the voice!" Kellie jumped in and protested. "Read it properly, with the spooky voice!"

I took a deep breath and started again. This spell was only about six sentences long but the way my friends were going it would take me till Christmas to finish reading it out.

"'Place these three vital elements into a piece of soft, clean white cloth—'"

"Huh? But where would you get—"

I shot Jen a shut-up look and carried on, louder.

"'—and fold the cloth gently over them. Hold this sacred package in your left hand and close your eyes. Visualize a cloak of white light settling on your shoulders. Now the spell is done, you will be irresistible to everyone you meet till the clock strikes 12 on the following night.'"

"Brilliant!" Chloe clapped her hands. "Let's all do it tonight! We can phone each other on Sunday and compare notes and see who got the most boys falling for them!"

"Uh-uh." Salma shook her head. "I'm taking my sisters and my niece to a birthday party tomorrow afternoon. If I do the spell tonight, that means that I risk having about 20 three-year-old boys fall in love with me. And frankly, I'm hoping for a boyfriend who's a little bit older than that."

"OK," Chloe shrugged. "Well, let's all do it over the weekend sometime and we'll meet up on Monday and see—"

"That's Mum!" Kellie suddenly yelped, her eyes wide and white with alarm, which was very odd seeing as Kellie and her mum were as big buddies as mums and daughters can get. "Quick, Ally! Hide the book! Mum'll freak if she sees that!"

"How come?" I frowned, stuffing the book down the back of my shorts in a panic and pulling my T-shirt down over the bump.

"You know how religious she is!" Kellie hissed. "She's dead against the idea of spells and stuff, even when it's only for a laugh!"

True. Mrs Vincent is one laid-back lady who lets Kellie watch just about anything on telly, except *Sabrina the Teenage Witch* and *Buffy the Vampire Slayer*. Yeah, now Buffy – *that* can be kind of behind-the-sofa scary sometimes, but Sabrina? She's about as satanic as marshmallow. Still, Kellie's mum's attitude to all things spooksome explained why Kellie was so jumpy when she was about to show us the book earlier.

"Hello, girls!" Mrs Vincent called out cheerfully, as she negotiated her way from the front door to the kitchen with about a hundred overflowing carrier bags, stuffed with great food. (You'd think she had to feed the entire cast and crew of *EastEnders* instead of one skinny daughter.)

But she didn't get a chance to appreciate our raggedy chorus of hellos back – the phone began to trill in the hall and she was too busy answering that to spot the five honest-we're-not-guilty faces in her living room.

"Where is it?" Kellie hissed in my direction.

"Down my shorts!" I hissed back, which set Jen off giggling. Till she saw Mrs Vincent's distraught expression in the doorway.

"Ally?" Kellie's mum called to me softly. "There's a call for you – it's your sister Linn. She says you're late for the funeral…"

"Omigod! Stanley! I completely forgot!" I gasped, slapping my hands over my mouth.

"There, there, dear…" Mrs Vincent came bustling over, ready to grasp me into her comfortingly large bosom.

Just as I felt myself being enveloped, I made out

Kellie's muffled voice saying, "Mum! Stanley's their *goldfish*!", and I was suddenly released.

"Your goldfish, huh?" she gazed down at me, her dark eyebrows shooting halfway up her forehead in surprise.

"My brother's," I shrugged. "He's pretty cut up about it."

"Well, I'll say a little prayer for Stanley, then," Mrs Vincent smiled indulgently.

"Thanks…"

As I hurried to the phone to talk to Linn, I couldn't help wondering what sort of prayer you could say for a goldfish. "*Our goldfish, who art in pond heaven…*"

"Hello? Linn?"

"Ally, you have exactly *five* minutes to get round here or I'll be burying you right next to Stanley."

Ah, Linn – I think some evil witch must have cast a "Totally, Utterly Grouchy" spell on her at birth…

Chapter 2

STANLEY THE GOLDFISH, RIP

The funeral of Stanley the goldfish had pulled a good crowd. As I burst into our back garden, panting, I spotted Tor (natch), Dad (on a late lunch-break), Linn (giving me one of her where-have-you-been? looks), Rowan (dressed especially spectacularly), Grandma and her boyfriend Stanley (the alive person, not the dead goldfish), Harry (our next-door neighbour) and some kid I'd never seen before in my life.

"Sorry I'm late!" I gasped at Tor in particular.

This funeral was all for Tor's sake. He'd always known that Stanley the goldfish's days were numbered – considering he had an unhealthy-looking lump on his side the size of a whole other goldfish – but finding Stanley floating at the top of his bowl last night had still come as a terrible shock to him. We all knew just by looking at him that Stanley was dead as a very dead fish, but just to put Tor's mind at rest, we asked Michael the vet from next door if he could come through and give his professional opinion. I think Tor was hoping Michael could work miracles and do a little mouth-to-mouth resuscitation, or have a pair of those zappy paddle things they use on *ER* to shock people's hearts into beating again. But there were no miracles; there was no mouth-to-mouth resuscitation; there were no miniature zappy paddle things. All there was was the horrible truth; it was all over for Stanley. There was nothing more we could do than plan a grand send-off for him, surrounded by everyone who knew and (sort of) loved him. *And* some weird little kid I'd never seen before.

"Um, well, now everyone's here, I guess I should say a few words..." Dad began, as we all gathered over by the newly dug hole by the back wall (the little kid too, even though he seemed *well* confused). "Stanley wasn't with us very long, but in that short time..."

I found myself tuning out what Dad was saying – I was too busy wondering why Tor was holding a small, gift-wrapped, ribbon-tied box in his hands. Had someone bought him a present to cheer him up at this time of his sad loss?

"...and I'm sure he'll have many happy days in pet heaven, swimming with other beautiful tropical fish—"

"But not sharks, Dad!" a forlorn Tor interrupted quickly, hugging his unopened present.

I guess Tor didn't want Stanley to get eaten as soon as he swam his way into pet heaven.

"OK, so lots of beautiful tropical fish, but no sharks," Dad continued solemnly. "Anyway, as I was saying…"

Next I got distracted by Rowan, who was starting to blub quietly. The blubbing wasn't a big surprise – Rowan can turn on the waterworks at the drop of a hankie – it was just the fact that in her long deep purple dress, mismatching crimson velvet choker and black fingerless gloves she looked like she'd come to the funeral of a member of the Addams family, not a pet fish. She'd even stuck a fake white lily (99p from the Pound Shop in Wood Green I found out later) in her longish, wavyish hair. The only thing that spoiled her theatrically sombre look was the two-tone colour of her hair – most of it was dyed dark blacky-brown, but there was a four-centimetre stripe of lighter brown along her parting where her true colour was growing back in. It looked bizarre; as if someone from the council had painted a road marking across the top of her head by accident. I could see Grandma staring disapprovingly at it now, and she wasn't the only one staring at my ditzy sister – the strange little kid seemed fixated by her.

"And now, at Tor's request," I heard Dad say, "we're going to sing the hymn 'All Things Bright and Beautiful'."

I was sure I heard Linn mumble "Urgh..." under her breath at that, but by the time I turned to look at her she was already belting out the words, keen as everyone to show Tor her support.

As we all warbled away (with the exception of the strange kid), Tor did the weirdest thing – he bent down and placed his present ever so gently into the hole in the ground. Doh! It was only then that it finally dawned on me that the ribbon-wrapped present was none other than Stanley's personalized coffin...

When the song finished, Dad crouched down beside Tor and began to brush the pile of earth at the side of the hole in to cover the top of the gift-wrapped coffin, while at the same time trying to push a curious, frantically-sniffing Rolf away from what was going on.

"Here," said Stanley (the alive person, not the dead goldfish), passing Dad a tiny something. "I made this for him."

Aw... Grandma's boyfriend had carved his namesake a tiny wooden cross, with "Stan" written on it in bottle-green paint. (It was a very small cross. I guess there wasn't room for the "-ley" part of his name.)

"And *I* made this, as a sort of memorial statuette!" sniffled Rowan, pulling a customized plastic doll out of her pocket, which was wearing a hand-made glittery mermaid's tail. The strange little kid's eyes flashed with something very close to panic when he saw that.

"Thank you," whispered Tor, leaning Rowan's effort up against the cross that Dad had just placed in the soft earth.

"And this is from Michael – he'd have loved to have been here if he hadn't had to be at work," said Harry, bending down and putting a beautiful pinky white conch shell down by the mermaid and the cross. "We got it when we were on holiday in Bali. Maybe Stanley will be swimming through lots of shells just like it wherever he is now."

Uh-oh. Harry was only trying to be nice, but those sweet words set Tor and Rowan off, and there were fountains of tears dribbling down both their cheeks. Now, the strange little kid was looking *seriously* worried.

"OK! That was a lovely funeral – but now it's time for cake. Come on, everybody into the kitchen, please!" Grandma said brightly, clapping her hands to get everyone's attention before the afternoon got any more morbid.

"Who's the kid?" I whispered to Linn, while Grandma shepherded everyone else through the back door of our house.

"Amir – he's an Afghani refugee that Tor met at that summer club thing he's going to," Linn explained, while dragging Rolf by the collar away from the recent burial site.

"Have you noticed the way he's been staring at Rowan?" I whispered, as we followed the others towards the house, and the party food that Grandma had laid out in an effort to brighten the proceedings.

"Yes. Guess you can't blame him for staring. I bet they don't have anyone who looks quite like Rowan where he's from."

"We should get Tor to ask him what's up, though."

"No point – he can't speak any English yet."

Ahh ... well, that made sense – Amir and Tor being mates, I mean. As a boy who never liked to say much of anything, the fact that Amir didn't speak the language wouldn't have mattered one tiny bit to our brother.

"Come on, you two!" Grandma chided me and Linn to hurry up. "You don't want all the food to get eaten because you're too busy dawdling!"

Gentle narking; that's just Grandma's way of talking, really. And we could see why she was hurrying us as soon as we got in the kitchen – Dad was pulling on his jacket and scooting back to work, casting a worried look in our direction and giving us a quick thumbs-up at the same time. Looked like Operation Cheer Tor Up was in our hands...

"Mmm! Lovely ice-cream, Grandma!" Rowan tried to enthuse brightly, even though her recent bout of blubbing had sent her mascara sliding south in frankly scary spidery lines.

Amir, I noticed, had been warily poking the green jelly alongside the ice-cream in his bowl up till that point, but as soon as Rowan spoke, he fixed his frowning eyes on her.

"So, Tor," I smiled, helping myself to a fairy cake drizzled in multicoloured icing sugar sprinkles, "Linn was telling me you met Amir at your summer club?"

Smart move, I thought – get him off the subject of death, goldfish and in particular, dead goldfish.

"Summer craft class," Tor corrected me.

"OK, whatever," I shrugged. "So..."

I was just about to ask some pertinent question about how long Amir had been in London, leading up to the question I was desperate to ask – did Amir have a clue what was going on today? (Um ...

some people buried a present in a garden and then ate food that wobbled, more like.) But just at that moment Amir started whispering frantically in Tor's ear, all the while staring sideways at Rowan. (Who didn't even notice, she was too busy helping herself to more raspberry ripple ice-cream.)

"What's Amir saying?" Linn asked Tor, settling herself down at the table.

"Don't know exactly," Tor shrugged. "Something about how Rowan's a witch. Or an alien. Or mad or something."

"What?" squealed Rowan. "I am *not*!"

I don't know, Tor might not be able to speak fluent Afghani or whatever the official language of Afghanistan is called, but I think his sixth sense tuned in pretty accurately to what Amir was thinking.

Actually, it was just as well Tor's sixth sense was being currently used to decipher Amir's words – at least that meant he wasn't aware of what was going on behind him at the back door.

From where I was sitting I could see Stanley (the alive person, not the dead goldfish) stroll casually out of the back door as if he was getting some air – then spotted him through the window *racing* across the lawn and trying to wrestle the newly dug-up gift-wrapped parcel from Winslet's determined jaws.

Stanley the goldfish, RIP.

I'm sorry – rest in peace? The way *our* dogs like to dig? I don't *think* so...

Chapter 3

SPOOKY SCRATCH-SCRATCHING

"Ow!" I gasped, as I accidentally yanked more than one hair out of my head.

Oh, yes; it was five to midnight – i.e. five to spell-time.

After a busy day hanging out with my friends, being prickled by mean cacti, burying goldfish and keeping Tor's spirits up (six bits of cake and three games of Mousetrap in a row managed to take his mind off the day's trauma) I was well and truly pooped. But since I overheard Linn at teatime say something about her mate Alfie (my boyfriend – in a parallel universe) popping round tomorrow night, nothing – not even acute pooped-ness – was going to stop me from trying out the "Totally, Utterly Charming Charm" tonight. Not even the fact that quarter of an hour ago I suddenly realized I had none of the vital spell-making stuff was going to stop me.

Still, after a bit of improvisation, I was almost there. I had the soft, clean piece of white material (my best knickers, straight out of the tumble-drier earlier today); I had the shell (there was still mud between my toes from sneaking out barefoot and in my PJs to borrow Stanley's memorial conch ten minutes ago); and now I had a hair from my head. (Make that *ten* hairs from my head. Um, would that make the spell ten times more powerful, I wondered?)

So now I had everything, I could get started. Except – drat – for the nutmeg. I'd totally forgotten about that ... and I really didn't think I'd ever seen any in the kitchen cupboards. The only spicy stuff we had was chilli powder. Would that do? It would have to...

"Arrghh!"

"Arrghh!" is the noise you make when you eat something that's made with too much chilli (i.e. probably something Rowan's cooked). But "Arrghh!" is *also* the noise you make when you quietly open your bedroom door at five-to-midnight – just as you're all set to tiptoe down to the kitchen – and find a small, ashen-faced spook-kid right outside it.

"Tor! What's up?" I whispered, hoping I hadn't woken Linn across the attic landing with my startled "Arrghh!" roar. "Did you have one of your nightmares?"

Tor has nightmares quite often. It's pretty hard

to work out what they're about, since he doesn't like describing them when they happen and then forgets all about them by morning. All I know is that when he gets them, it's *my* room he sneaks up to, and in the morning – when I wake up with a dead arm where he's been sleeping on it, and frozen stiff, since he's somehow managed to cocoon himself in the entire duvet – Tor is bright as a very bright button while *I* feel like a one-armed grouchy bear that's been woken out of hibernation too soon.

"No, not a nightmare," Tor shook his head, padding straight past me at top speed, clutching half the soft-toy collection off his bed.

"Well, what's wrong then?" I asked, pausing before I closed the door to let a cat that wasn't Colin slink in behind him.

"Noises," said Tor vaguely, wriggling himself deep down under the safety of my duvet. Only the top of his head, half of Mr Penguin and the arm of a fluffy sloth were sticking out. With a boy and toy mound in my bed and a cat that wasn't Colin presently curling itself contentedly on my pillow, I wasn't entirely sure if there was going to be room for me in there.

"What kind of noises?" I asked, scooping the *Lovey-Dovey Spells* book, my clean white knickers, the conch shell and my clump of hair off the floor ffing them hastily into the nearest drawer. ...dn't think Tor would appreciate Stanley's ...ve being desecrated so soon – i.e. having his memorial conch shell wrapped up in my knickers.)

"Tapping. And scratching. And some more tapping," Tor mumbled.

With a quick glance at the clock – two minutes to midnight – I knew my chance to charm Alfie tomorrow was now *well* out the window. Ho hum. Still, the spell would keep for another day – and I might even spend a little of my allowance tomorrow on nutmeg to make the thing work properly. I mean, who knows what effect chilli might have had? Maybe it would have made everyone totally, utterly hacked off with me, instead of totally, utterly charmed. And anyway, how could I ever get bugged by someone as adorable as Tor? Putting thoughts of spells and spice and clean knickers out of my head, I went over and perched myself on the few centimetres of bed space that weren't already taken and patted Tor through the thickness of my cloud-covered duvet.

"Look, I'm sure you were just having a nightmare, Tor," I tried to assure him. "It's been an upsetting day, with Stanley's funeral and everything, and I think you probably just heard all the normal noises in your room, only in your nightmare they sounded *weird* or something."

That's the thing – Tor's room at night is a world of creaking, scuffling and whirring, as all the endless small beasties in their cages go about their nocturnal business.

"It *wasn't* normal noises!" came a muffled protest. "It was different! It was scary!"

For a second, I wondered guiltily if what he'd heard was me sneaking out for the conch shell and sneaking back in. But I knew I'd been as quiet as a particularly silent mouse, with only the faintest clunk of the back door lock and the tiniest squeak of the loose floorboard I'd stepped on outside Rowan's room to give me away. I certainly hadn't done any tap-tapping or scratch-scratching that I could remember.

"I'm scared, Ally…"

Two Malteser eyes, round and brown, peeked over the edge of the duvet. Nothing I could say tonight was going to calm him down – only a cuddle would help.

"OK, budge up!" I said cheerfully, squishing a fat elephant further down the bed so there was a tiny strip for me to lie on. "Now close your eyes and think of nice things, and I'll stick the light out!"

I don't know what nice things Tor thought of (patting animals, and meeting Rolf Harris in person, probably), but whatever it was, I could tell from his breathing that he was asleep in about two seconds.

Which left me wide awake (and uncomfortable), listening to the far-off midnight chimes of church bells. *And* listening out with every nerve-ending in my body for any spooky tapping and scratching noises coming up the attic stairs...

Chapter 4

THE MYSTERY OF THE GNOMES...

"Listen to this! This is brilliant!" Dad laughed, his eyes fixed on the headlines of the local paper that had just flopped through our front door this Saturday morning.

"You'll be late opening the shop!" Linn frowned at him, as she shoved her hairbrush in her bag and got ready to leave for her summer job at the posh clothes shop up on Crouch Hill.

"Yeah, yeah," Dad grinned at her, wafting the paper in one hand and a piece of toast and marmalade in the other. "I'll get there and there'll be *queues* of people with bikes all around the block, *desperate* for me to open so they can buy a puncture-repair kit!"

Linn rolled her perfectly made-up eyes at the ceiling and tutted. For a second there, she looked exactly the same as Grandma (apart from the make-up of course) – it was just the identical despairing look that comes over our gran's face when she realizes she isn't going to get any sense out of us.

"*What's* brilliant, Dad?" asked Tor, gazing up from his chequerboard toast (he'd alternated wobbly squares of marmalade with wobbly squares of Marmite and seemed to be more interested in staring at its perfect-ish symmetry than actually eating it).

"This!" Dad smiled, setting himself down on a chair as Linn snapped her bag shut with a snippy click. "Wait for it; here's the headline: *There's No Place Like Gnome!*"

"Gnomes? Like as in garden gnomes?" I wrinkled my nose at him, wondering what exactly he was on about. But then my brain wasn't really working properly this morning despite the two coffees I'd already had (that's what lack of sleep on a ten-centimetre strip of bed does for you).

"Yeah!" Dad nodded his cropped head of hair. "It says here that all these snooty people in a street in Muswell Hill are in a right strop because their gnomes and garden ornaments keep moving around to other gardens in the night!"

"You mean some idiot's nicking them," said Linn disapprovingly, as she headed out into the hall.

"No, they're not *nicking* them – they're only moving them around for a laugh, like an April fool!" Dad called out after her. "See? It says here that a Mrs Montgomery came out of the house yesterday morning to find her pottery hedgehog three doors up on someone's bird table while she'd got a mystery gnome taking a head-first dive into her ornamental pond!"

"*Still* sounds like nicking to me! See you later...!" Linn voice trailed off as we heard her pull open the front door.

"Well, I suppose it *isn't* a very nice thing to do..." Dad muttered sheepishly, now that Linn had chastised him.

"Well, it is *quite* funny," I grinned wickedly.

"Yeah!" Tor butted in, too.

"It is, isn't it?" Dad sniggered like a kid, looking all of a sudden exactly like Tor, only with stubble.

"What is what?" asked a voice in the kitchen doorway. It wasn't Rowan – she was still well and truly zonked out upstairs in her raspberry-painted room. (Rowan thinks the only reason to get up before eleven on a non-school day is if the house was on fire...)

"Never mind what is what," I spluttered at the sight of my friend Kyra walking into the room like she lived here. "Where did you come from?"

"Your front door!" Kyra replied sarkily, raising one side of her top lip. "Your sister let me in! Hi, Mr Love! Hi, Tor!"

For my brother and Dad, Kyra dropped the sarcasm and beamed a winning smile.

"Yeah, but it's only half-nine," I pointed out. "Don't you have stuff to do at this time on a Saturday? Like mooch around or watch some telly?"

What I really meant was, how about leaving it for a while and coming around when a person might be dressed? Or maybe using that strange modern invention they call the "phone" to call ahead and warn people that you're dropping by?

"Well, I got bored," shrugged Kyra, reaching out and helping herself to a piece of toast from the pile on the plate in front of her.

"Hey, I'll leave you girls to it," said Dad, screeching his chair back and flopping the paper on the table. "See you later!"

And with a quick ruffle of his toast-crumbed fingers in Tor's hair, Dad was off, to deal with the legions of bike-owners who'd be waiting impatiently for him round at the shop. (Ha!)

"Nice pyjamas," Kyra nodded at Tor's *Spiderman* favourites. "Nicer than your sister's, anyway."

Tor grinned, showing off his mixed set of diddy baby teeth and partly grown big teeth.

"Look, I wasn't exactly expecting visitors, OK?" I frowned, self-consciously pulling my ratty old T-shirt down over a luminous pair of stripy Lycra cycling shorts I'd never be caught dead in outside. "So how come you're *really* here this early?"

Something had to be up. Something was *always* up with Kyra.

"I phoned Salma last night – she said you've got a spell book!" said Kyra, sitting up straight from her slouch and getting straight to the point.

"Well, for a start, it's not *my* book – it's Kellie's – and anyway, it's not like it's a proper spell book: it's just a dumb thing for fun."

The reason I was quick to jump in like that was because I wasn't exactly thrilled about the idea of Tor getting it into his head that one of his sisters really *was* a witch (i.e. me), as opposed to just *dressing* like one (i.e. Rowan). He had enough strange things to have nightmares about, and I didn't want to add the vision of me casting spells to all the tappings and scratchings that were currently giving him goosebumps.

Not that Tor seemed to be listening to Kyra – he was too wrapped up in cutting his toast into tiny squares and feeding the Marmite pieces to something under the table.

"Who *cares* whose book it is?" Kyra shrugged in her usual infuriatingly casual way. "Just give us a look – I really, really need some help with my non-existent love life…"

"Sam still not phoned yet?" I asked, conveniently forgetting the fact that she was irritating now that we'd touched on some gossip. Sam was this boy she'd met on holiday a couple of weeks ago. After wall-to-wall snogging sessions whenever their parents weren't looking, Kyra thought she was all set to have a tanned and cool boyfriend when she came back to London. But they do say holiday romances never last, and even though Sam only lived in South London, it might as well have been Mars for all the contact she'd had with him.

"*Three* chances, that's all I said I'd give him," Kyra announced dramatically, holding up her fingers for emphasis.

"Kyra, that's six fingers," I nodded towards her hands. "How many chances did you give him exactly?"

Kyra wrinkled her freckly brown nose and added another finger for good measure.

"You've left *seven* messages on his mobile?"

She nodded slowly, looking sheepish.

"So, see? I really need help! Can I get a look at the book, Ally? Please?!"

I glanced over at Tor, who was now spoon-feeding Marmite straight out of the jar and into whoever's waiting jaws were under the table, and decided it was safe to leave him in Kyra's company for the few minutes it would take to get the book from my bedroom and pull on a pair of jeans.

"Try and cheer him up," I whispered above the buzz of the song blasting out on Radio One. "He had a rotten day yesterday."

"No problem!" the queen of shrugs shrugged once more.

"Cheer him up," I'd said.

"No problem!" she'd said.

Ha!

When I walked back into the kitchen I found Kyra leaning over Tor with a frilly-edged sheet draped over her, making very weird growling noises. Oh, no – my mistake – the growling was coming from Winslet under the table, who really, *really* didn't like the frilly apparition too much judging from the way she'd locked her teeth on to the corner of the sheet and was trying to rip it to shreds.

"What's going on?" I frowned.

"I told Kyra about the tapping," Tor jabbered, jumping up from his seat excitedly, "and she says we've got a polterghost!"

"*Geist!* Polter*geist!*" laughed Kyra, hauling the sheet off her head, the wiry curls of her high ponytail springing back into place.

"Kyra!" I hissed, trying to dislocate Winslet's jaws from the sheet so it could be returned to the laundry basket where it belonged. "Don't go telling him spooky stuff like that!"

"Why not? It's just a bit of fun – like that *Lovey-Dovey Spells* book!"

Good grief, did she need it explained in minute detail? It was like this: if the spell worked, the worst that could happen was that your dream boy fell splat-bang hopelessly in love with you (pretty excellent really). If Tor believed the poltergeist theory, then the worst that could happen was that he'd be so freaked out he'd end up sleeping in my bed for the next three *years*.

And *that*, Kyra Davies, would certainly not be fun...

Chapter 5

UPSIDE-DOWN BEANS AND POLTERGHOSTS

"Poltergeist: a spirit believed to be responsible for noises and acts of mischief, such as throwing objects about."

So, in other words, a ghost that's into practical jokes. I'd looked that up in the dictionary yesterday, after Kyra left (and as soon as I'd got Tor settled in front of his much-loved video of *The Lion King* to take his mind off all things polterghostly). But you know something? Some weird things have happened the past couple of days. Like last night, I went into the hall and realized that one of Mum's paintings had been turned upside down. And that wasn't the *only* thing that was upside down – Grandma's very into stacking tins in the kitchen cupboard hyper-neatly, with all labels facing out (she could win a Neat Cupboard Contest *easy*, if there was ever anyone nuts enough to invent such a thing), but when Dad went to grab a tin of beans for breakfast this morning, every single can was standing on its head. And don't ask me how

Rowan's set of front-door keys ended up in the freezer. I mean, I know Winslet's pretty bad at nicking stuff and stashing it in strange places, but having no thumbs, I think she'd have struggled a bit to pull the door open. And even standing on Rolf's back, she'd never have been able to reach Mum's painting or the kitchen cupboard.

Anyway, enough of upside-down beans and polterghosts; I had more pressing worries, like quite how late Tor was going to make us this morning, and if Rolf was going to need his nose stitched...

Poor Rolf. He looked like he'd been in a fight with a cat and lost. Actually he *had* been in a fight with a cat and lost.

OK, OK, from Rolf's side, it *hadn't* been a fight – all he'd wanted to do was sniff the cat, even possibly *lick* the cat to see what flavour it was (i.e. not one of ours) – but the cat took it all wrong and presumed it was about to be eaten. Taking no chances it did some mean karate moves in the blink of an eye and ended up lacerating poor Rolf's nose with its specially sharpened, dog-slashing claws.

I say poor Rolf, but two seconds after the incident, once I'd dabbed his nose for a bit with a ratty old tissue from my pocket, he seemed to have bravely (stupidly?) forgotten about the pain and was getting back on with the serious business of yanking my arm to breaking point as he lunged on the end of his lead towards the park. And Winslet may have been a whole lot smaller than Rolf, but inside that small, hairy body was a Sherman tank judging from the pulling power she had at the end of her own lead.

"Tor!" I groaned, sensing I'd lost my brother yet again to the lure of a cat. That's the trouble with Tor – a ten-minute walk to the park turns into a half-hour neighbourhood cat-patting session. He's always the same, and it doesn't matter that he's got five cats to pat at home, *or* that one of these doorstep-draped moggies had just assaulted Rolf (Tor had hugged the cat, then Rolf), the cat-patting was just too much of a ritual to break.

"Coming!" Tor shouted at me from four houses back.

But he was *plainly* not coming – not the way the latest cat he'd found was rolling on its back happily letting Tor rub its tummy. You know, I kind of wished that Tor hadn't said he wanted to come along today on my regular Sunday morning dog walk with Billy. For a start, Billy and me always used this get-together to catch up on what'd happened in our lives that week, and part of what had happened in *my* life this week was a fair amount of spookiness that I didn't want to bring up in front of Tor. Second, Tor's inevitable cat-patting along the way meant we were pretty late for Billy, and although the park entrance was tantalizingly close now (as a blindfolded person could tell from the way the dogs were pulling and whining), the bench I always meet Billy on was up at the top of the hill, near Alexandra Palace itself. If we tried running up that slope in a hurry, I wouldn't have enough oxygen left in my body to talk to Billy for at least an hour.

I was just mulling this over (while having my arms gently jerked out of their sockets by Rolf and Winslet) when a small blur of boy went streaking past me towards the park entrance.

"Race you!" yelled Tor, as I felt myself being lifted off my feet and dragged along the pavement by the sheer force of four sets of determined paws. (I think there's got to be some husky in both their mongrel mix somewhere. Although I can't see either of them being expert sledge dogs – Rolf would keep wanting to run off and bark at penguins and Winslet would just gnaw through the reins.)

As soon as we'd whizzed into the park and the dogs set their eyes on the acres of green in front of them, they stood stock-still, waiting impatiently for me to let them off their leads. For a second, I toyed with the idea of keeping their leads on, and letting them pull me bodily up the hill, but then I decided that excellent idea as it was, a) the dogs would take the more exciting waist-high route through the bramble bushes (and I had enough scratches on my legs thanks to Kellie's cacti) and b) it was kind of cruel…

Anyway, it turned out that we didn't have to trawl all the way up the hill to meet Billy after all – I'd just spotted him running down the slope in our direction. Correction: running down the slope in the direction of this large, marshy puddle quite close to us. All dogs who get walked around Ally Pally fall instantly in love with this permanent puddle. You can tell the ones who've recently checked it out by the black pairs of muddy "socks" they're wearing and the contented smiles on their doggy faces.

"Is that Precious?" Tor asked, turning and squinting at me as the sun dazzled his eyes.

"No," I shook my head as I gazed at the all-black terrier thing that was emerging from the mud-hole.

"Precioussssss! *Noooooo!*" roared Billy, setting eyes on the black terrier and slowing his run to a gentle flail of his gangly arms and legs.

"*Yapppitttty-yappppitttttty-yappppppittttty-yap!*"

Uh-oh – that irritating, ear-splitting bark could only belong to one dog. And as Precious – the normally white poodle – completely ignored her owner and came bounding over to greet Rolf and Winslet, shedding blobs of flying mud as he ran, I knew Billy's neat-freak mum was going to absolutely *kill* him when he went home. I could see the headlines now: *"Mum Strangles Son with Dettol-Scented Rubber Gloves! Police investigators said muddy dog rolling on new cream carpets pushed her over the edge…"*

"…and then *there* she is, with a frilly sheet over her head, making *Scooby Doo* noises and wiffling on about poltergeists!"

I was filling Billy in with Kyra's classic case of brother-frightening, as the brother in question went tearing off way ahead of us, like a token member of Rolf, Winslet and Precious's doggy pack.

"But poltergeists *do* exist, Ally!"

"Yeah, and Santa Claus is this *real* bloke who watches telly 364 days of the year then flies through the sky for one night only, delivering presents to zillions of kids!"

I rolled my eyes, wondering why on earth I'd expected Billy of all people to be rational and sensible about the poltergeist issue, or *anything* really.

"What d'you mean? Are you saying Santa *doesn't* exist?" said Billy mournfully.

I turned to give him a you've-got-to-be-kidding! stunned look, when I saw from his wall-to-wall grin that he *was* kidding.

"Aw, come on, Ally! I didn't *really* have you going there, did I? I mean, no one over the age of *five* believes in Santa Claus. Except for Sandie, maybe..."

OK, that deserved a small punch in the arm. Billy never misses an opportunity to take the mickey out of my other best friend, whether she's around to hear it or not. Yes, Sandie's a bit of a softie, but there's nothing wrong with that. It's better than being a berk like Billy.

"Ow!" he whined, rubbing his arm (though I could see he was still grinning, annoyingly). "What was that for?"

"Not having anything nice to say about Sandie, ever." I narrowed my eyes at him.

Suitably chastised, Billy dropped his gaze to the patchy grass in front of us and shut up for a second or two. When he spoke again, it wasn't to apologize – he just changed the subject back to all things spooksome. He probably sussed that was the safest option (i.e. I wouldn't thump him again). God, I just wish my two best mates could get along better, instead of treating each other like aliens from different planets (the planet Berk and the planet Softie...).

"Anyhow, Ally, how can you say poltergeists don't exist, when you just told me weird stuff has been happening in your house?"

"It wasn't *much* weird stuff," I shrugged, "and anyway, Dad said maybe Grandma did it all by accident on Friday, 'cause she was in a bit of a mad rush getting all the party things together for Stanley's funeral."

"So ... *you're* saying that your grandma was *dusting* the picture, and accidentally hung it back up, but upside down?" Billy asked dubiously.

"Well, yeah, *maybe* ... and we just didn't spot it till last night."

"And then she *forgetfully* went into the kitchen cupboard and put every tin in the wrong way round?"

"Um – well, *possibly*. I mean—"

"And then she took Rowan's keys and put them in the freezer, all because she was thinking about what flavour *jelly* to make?"

You know, when Billy put it like that it really did sound kind of unlikely.

"Come on, Ally! There's about as much chance of your gran doing all that stuff as there is of my mum laughing when I take Precious home in the state he's in!"

Hmm ... I could see his point.

"But what else could it be?" I frowned, annoyed with him for dumping cold water over Dad's reassuring theory.

"It's like Kyra says!" Billy insisted, pushing his baseball cap further back on his head. "It's a poltergeist!"

"Oh, yeah? And how come you're such an expert on poltergeists all of a sudden?"

"I'm just reading this horror book with one in it!" he began blabbering excitedly. "See, there's this family move to these woods in America and they don't know there's been a really gory murder there and then all this stuff starts happening and littlest kid gets sucked into this vortex in the basement and—"

"Stop!" I interrupted, holding my hand up in front of his stupid face. "Billy, what exactly are you trying to tell me?"

"Well..." he blinked, looking confused. "It's a story about—"

"That's it – it's a *story*, Billy! A made-up *story*! I want *hard* evidence, not the plot of the latest book you got out of the library!"

"Hey, if you want *evidence*," he said defensively,

"then just read the local papers! There's *plenty* of spook stuff going on round Ally Pally just now!"

"Like what?"

Up ahead, I could see all four dogs (I'm including Tor in that) rolling about in some newly cut grass. When Tor, Winslet and Rolf stood back up, they shook the grass off themselves. In the case of Precious, the grass just stuck to the mud. From a distance, he looked like a large chocolate truffle covered in green icing-sugar sprinkles.

"Like all that stuff about the garden gnomes and everything moving about in the night!" Billy blurted out. "Have you heard about that?"

"Yes, course I have! But that's just some kids mucking around!"

"Ah, but *is* it?" Billy waggled his finger in my face. "It *could* be magic! I mean, this whole area is on ley-lines and they're very cosmic and mysterious and everything! Maybe there're strange things happening all over the whole area!"

I didn't want to believe a word of what Billy was wittering, but I couldn't help feeling a shiver slither up my spine. You know, all this spook stuff had started happening since Friday; since Kellie bought that spell book. Maybe her mum was right after all – maybe there *was* something wrong with messing around with that kind of thing, even if it *was* just for a laugh...

"Hey, Ally, I was thinking..." Billy suddenly said, in a sombre voice.

Uh-oh, I didn't know if I could handle him telling me any more weirdy-beardy facts.

"What?" I asked warily.

"Can I come back to yours?"

"Why?"

Did he want to check for signs of poltergeist disturbance for himself?

"My mum'll go nuts if I take Precious home like that. Can I give him at bath at yours?"

"Sure." I nodded without hesitation.

After all, if there *was* a poltergeist hanging around at our place, five minutes of listening to Precious yappitty-yapping and it'd surely give up messing with our cupboards and spook off to another, much quieter house (pretty please)...

THE "HOW TO FAIL" SPELL...

I was still clearing specks of mud off the red-painted walls of our bathroom when the girls arrived on Monday afternoon.

I thought me and Billy had done an OK job of tidying up yesterday, after the trauma of washing Precious (you'd think we were trying to *dissect* him instead of *wash* him from the howling hysterics he had). But of course when Grandma turned up this morning she'd noticed every speckle of mud we'd missed.

"What happened in here?" she'd asked me, after calling for me to come and inspect the damage. "I don't remember seeing anything on the weather forecast about indoor tornadoes in the area!"

Urgh ... it wasn't just the mud splodges that Precious had sprayed over the walls, it was the fact that two of the overgrown plants in our greenhouse of a bathroom had branches bent and broken off them, from Billy's stupid dog's many attempts to scramble out of the bath to freedom.

"We were washing Precious – he was covered in mud," I'd explained.

"*That's* funny," Grandma frowned at me. "I was *sure* Billy had a bath in his *own* house!"

She sure can do a fine line in sarcasm, our gran...

As soon as I heard the doorbell, I peeled off my Marigolds and hurried downstairs.

"I'll finish tidying up later, honest!" I tried to reassure Grandma, who was heading out to the shops as all my friends tumbled in for our pre-arranged get-together.

The reason my gran looked at me warily there wasn't so much that she didn't believe that I'd finish cleaning the bathroom (I'd be too scared of her not to), but because she thought I'd gone slightly mad. But when she'd come up to check on me earlier, well, I'd just had to ask, didn't I?

"Uh, Grandma ... did you, um, do something funny with the tins in the kitchen cupboard on Friday?"

"Funny? No, of course I didn't do something funny with the tins! Why on earth would I do that? Now look – you've missed that paw-print halfway up the wall..."

After that, I didn't bother mentioning the picture or Rowan's keys.

With a few hello/goodbyes in my gran's

direction, all my friends piled into the house, heading straight for the comfort of our living room and its squashy sofa and chairs.

"Back in a sec!" Kyra darted past me in the direction of the loo.

"Hey! You can finish off my chores while you're in there!" I called after her as she disappeared up the stairs. "The tiles just need hosing down!"

"In your dreams!" she called back, slamming the bathroom door shut.

"So how was your holiday?" I asked Sandie, joining the others already sprawling themselves around the living room.

It was the first time I'd seen my best friend in nearly a week. Her big blue eyes looked even bigger and bluer than usual after getting a bit of a tan on her trip to the seaside.

"It was OK," she shrugged.

Sandie can sometimes say clunky things without meaning too, but generally she's too nice for her own good, and can never bring herself to say a bad word about anything, or anyone. So, translated, "It was OK" meant she'd had a pretty lousy time, I reckoned.

"Not much fun, then?" I asked her straight out.

"The place my great aunt lives in – it's pretty boring," Sandie shrugged, almost apologetically.

"And she's all right ... it's just that she's a bit ... bossy. And deaf."

Hmm. Shy Sandie and a bossy old woman who's too deaf to hear Sandie's shy little voice – that wasn't a great combination.

"She kept going on at Sandie's parents that they should name the new baby after her, if it's a girl," Chloe chipped in. She'd obviously heard all Sandie's sagas on the walk round here.

"What's your great-aunt's name?" I asked Sandie.

"Ethel," Sandie grimaced.

"*Ethel?*" shrieked Jen, as everyone collapsed into giggles.

"Still, it could have been worse!" I grinned.

"Worse how?" Sandie stared at me.

"She could have insisted they call the baby after her even if it was a boy!"

The best thing about having friends you've known for ever is that you all have the same sense of humour, and yes, ours is pretty pathetic, but at least it's nice that they laughed at my lame joke.

"Anyway, let's get on to the good stuff!" Chloe announced, once everyone had stopped sniggering at the idea of Sandie having a little brother called Ethel. "How did everyone get on with their spells?"

"Rubbish," said Salma, shaking off her slip-on

trainers and stretching out her long legs on the carpet to tickle a snoozing Colin on the tummy with her bare toes. "I did it exactly like you read out, Ally, but I didn't charm anyone. I was in Tesco with Mum all yesterday afternoon and not *one* gorgeous boy came anywhere near me."

"Me neither," said Kellie. "I tried it the last two nights, and nothing."

"It didn't work for me either," said Jen, all curled up on the beanbag.

"Yeah, that's 'cause you did it at eight o'clock at night, instead of midnight!" Chloe raised her eyebrows accusingly at Jen.

"Well, you *know* I can never stay awake that late!" Jen protested.

"What about you, Chloe? How did it go?" I asked her, before I got round to confessing that I hadn't even tried the spell yet, after Tor gatecrashing my room on Friday night.

"Great – I *thought*," began Chloe, stretching her arms over the back of the sofa. "I was in New Look in Wood Green with my mum on Saturday, and I kept seeing this really cute young guy checking me out. Everywhere I went, he'd kind of turn up beside me. Then I realized that he worked there, and he wasn't watching me 'cause he liked me – he thought I was a shoplifter!"

"Hey, *you'll* have to try the spell too, Sandie!" said Kellie enthusiastically, once everyone had stopped giggling at Chloe's sorry tale.

"No *way*!" Sandie widened her eyes in alarm. "I'd be *far* too scared. And knowing my luck, the first person I'd see after I did the spell would be our postman! Or ... or Billy, or someone stupid!"

She gave a little shudder at the very thought. Well, she had a point – her postman was about 50 and looked like he lived on a diet of pies, chips and Snicker bars from the size of him. And as for her and Billy, well, I'm sure I remember an episode of *Star Trek* where they said that inhabitants of the planets Berk and Softie were totally incompatible.

"Hey, you didn't start without me, did you?" Kyra huffed, coming back into the room and finding us all yakking madly about boys and love spells.

"Yeah, but don't worry – you didn't miss much," I grinned at her.

"Ally – is it OK if I go and get some Coke or something for everyone?" Sandie suddenly interrupted, turning into the perfect hostess, which was cool, since it saved me the trouble.

"Sure," I nodded.

"So what about you, Kyra? Charm any lads?"

Chloe smirked, as Kyra moved away from the door to let Sandie out.

"Certainly did!" Kyra broke into a beaming grin.

"Who? What? Tell, tell!" Kellie patted the edge of the armchair for Kyra to sit down.

"I did the spell on Saturday night," Kyra beamed, like the cat who'd got the cream, "and guess who phoned me yesterday?"

"Robbie Williams?" I suggested.

"Sam from my holiday!" she announced, totally blanking my flippant remark. "He finally phoned me back!"

"No!" gasped Jen. "What did he say?"

"Well, he said he'd love to—"

Who knows what Sam would have loved to do – we never found out, because Sandie came zooming into the living room as if she was being chased by an axe murderer.

"I-I've just— It was, oooh! It was like all ... I don't know!" she blurted out nothing that would give us a *clue* to what was wrong.

"What's up, Sand?" I frowned, striding over and rubbing her arm.

"I think I ... I ... just saw a ghost! I just looked out into the hall and it was ... floating up the stairs!"

For half a second, none of us said or did anything. Then bravery or curiosity or plain *madness* made me open the door and peer out into the hall and up the stairs.

"Can you see anything?" Jen squeaked breathlessly behind me.

"Uh, yes," I nodded, my heart rate slowing down to normal now that I'd caught sight of the apparition sitting on the first-floor landing. "Back in a sec..."

At the top of the stairs, the apparition began to growl softly.

"It's OK, babe," I said soothingly, tiptoeing up each step towards the bad-tempered ghost.

Now that I was closer, I could recognize more than just the four short paws that had given Winslet away when I first spotted her. Now I could see that she was wearing an interesting outfit made from taped-together pieces of white kitchen roll, with holes poked through for her eyes to see out and her hairy ears to stick up through.

"That's your dog!" I heard Chloe say indignantly from the safety of the living-room doorway down below. "How did she get all that stuff on her?"

You know, if my hideous cousin Charlie wasn't safely back home in Canada with his hideous twin sister and their equally hideous parents, I'd put a bet on this being his handiwork. But he wasn't here, and neither was anyone else in our family right now.

Omigod – was the poltergeist of Crouch End up to mischief again…?

Chapter 7

LET'S MEDITATE ... (PARP)

You could tell how bored I was from the fact that for the last half-hour, I'd been transfixed by Spartacus the tortoise eating a lettuce leaf (very, very slowly).

The half-hour before that, I'd sat in the deckchair, absently pulling at a loose thread and unravelling the bottom of one leg of my cut-off denim shorts until Grandma caught me doing it and told me to stop. (I'm glad she did – it wouldn't have looked too cool to have one leg of my shorts shorter than the other.)

The half-hour before *that* I'd been trying to help Grandma with the weeding, but I kept getting muddled up between what was a plant and what was a weed and before we ended up with a border full of spectacular weeds and nothing else, Grandma told me to go and do something more useful, like get out of her way.

Now that Spartacus and his mind-blowingly dull lettuce-munching had lost its attraction, I raised my eyes to see what Tor was currently up to. He and the dogs had been playing with a hula hoop last time I looked (i.e. Tor spun the hula hoop around his waist while the dogs went mental and tried to bite it as it whirled past their wet noses). But now he seemed to be trying to perfect a trapeze-style circus act by squeet-squeeting back and forth on the garden swing, while patting his legs and trying to encourage either of our two confused dogs to leap on to his lap as he swung.

Well, I guess I could watch this for half an hour, since there was nothing else to do...

"Hi."

"Oh, hi!" I turned and glanced up at Rowan, who was a vision of primary colours today, like a big tube of Smarties. "I thought you'd gone out!"

Like Linn, Rowan had had a summer job – sweeping up and making tea at a trendy hairdresser's in Camden – which *unlike* Linn, Rowan managed to do for about all of two minutes. Well, to be precise, it lasted as long as our horrible relatives from Canada were staying with us. As soon as they'd left and it was safe to be around the house again, she packed it in. I don't think Dad and Grandma minded that she hadn't stuck it out; in the short space of time she was there she'd managed to get herself a tattoo, and while that hadn't been too drastic (a life-sized ladybird on her arm) I think they were both kind of worried that if she'd carried on working there she might have come back with a pink mohican or a pierced nipple or something equally gruesome.

"I was supposed to be hanging out with Von today, but she blew me out," Rowan shrugged, watching Tor practise his so far very unsuccessful circus skills. (Rolf and Winslet were both sitting in front of him, their tails wagging and their heads bobbing back and forwards as he swung, but neither of them seemed to know what exactly he expected of them.)

"So, are you coming out to the garden, then?" I said, mildly pleased that Rowan could sit here in the sunshine with me and share my boredom.

Suddenly, as if she was doing a mime of being in a lift, Rowan bent her knees and slowly lowered herself down to my side.

"I kind of thought you could come inside with me. To my room," she whispered out of the corner of her mouth, her eyes still fixed on Tor.

"Why?" I asked in my normal voice.

"Just do it! I'll go first – you follow me in a minute so no one notices anything. All right?"

So no one notices? No one who? Who was remotely interested in whether either or both of us went inside the house for a bit?

Maybe it wasn't just mime that Rowan was practising for – maybe she was working up an audition piece for the role of a spy in the next James Bond movie...

I was too puzzled to say anything; I just watched her mime herself upright in her imaginary lift, then turn and disappear into the kitchen. For a second, I sat there staring at Grandma's bent back, as she happily tore up weeds while humming along to some song twiddling away on the portable radio by her side, then at an equally happy Tor, swooping away on his swing, and realized that neither of them had even noticed Rowan had been in the garden, never mind the fact that she'd gone back in again.

Still, her strange little pantomime was the most interesting thing that had happened all morning (not that *that* was saying much), so with only the slightest creak of my deckchair, I got up and quietly padded into the house after my weirdo sister. I'd just stepped into the coolness of the kitchen when a thunk and a roar (or was it more a roar then a thunk?) had me spinning around.

Aha – looked like Tor's circus training session had worked too well. I turned just quick enough to see both Rolf and Winslet do a synchronized leap on to Tor's lap, and all three tumble off the swing in a groaning, giggling, barking pile on the grass.

"Is he all right?" I called out to Grandma, who'd immediately hurried over to check for lumps, bumps and broken bones.

"Everyone's fine," Grandma called back in her usual practical voice, as she pulled Tor upright and tried to fend off grateful licks from Rolf.

Well, despite not having a safety net, everyone was OK in the garden. Which meant I could continue with my plan to find out what was going on – OK or otherwise – in Rowan's strange little world...

"You want me to do *what*?"

I stared at Rowan though the gloom. Despite blazing sunshine outside, she'd pulled her heavy (and holey) red velvet curtains closed, and instead of flicking on any of the little lamps or reams of fairy lights she has dotted or draped around her room, the only light (apart from tiny beams of sunlight cheekily sneaking through the holes and chinks in the curtains) was a circle of dainty tea-light candles she'd placed on an old tin tray in the middle of the carpet.

"Meditate!" Rowan nodded at me enthusiastically, sitting cross-legged on the other side of the tray of candles from me. "It's the only way we can get in touch!"

"Who says I *want* to get in touch with a poltergeist?"

I hadn't been the only one talking to friends about the weirdness going on around our place; Rowan had been spilling the spooky happenings to her mates Von and Chazza. Apparently Von had a top tip for sorting out pesky poltergeists – she'd read that if you meditate for a bit to clear your mind, then start asking questions into thin air, the poltergeist might just get back to you.

"But it's like Von says, that way, you could make contact!" Rowan tried to convince me. (You know something? It's very hard to take a girl seriously when she's trying to tell you about the supernatural if she's got her hair tied in bunches with little kids' strawberry-shaped bobbles, like Rowan had today.)

"*But,*" I retaliated, with my killer point, "*then* what? What do you chat about? 'Hi, Mr Poltergeist, just wondered what your plans are? How long do you think you'll be hanging around our house?' That sort of thing? '*Well*, girls, I *had* thought about sticking around and terrifying you all for a decade or two at *least!*'"

"Don't be silly! It wouldn't *be* like that!" said Rowan, with baffling certainty. Urm, since when had she become such an expert in the paranormal?

Hey, maybe our family could make a fortune selling her story straight to Hollywood, as a follow-up to *Buffy*. I could see it in the TV listings mags now: *Rowan the Poltergeist Slayer*.

"Well, what *would* it be like, Ro? Are you going to ask what its favourite colour is?" I frowned at my sister, figuring that maybe if I stared into her eyes long and hard enough, I'd be able to make out the bits of her brain that must have broken away and floated off around her head. "Are you going to ask it if it likes the way you've done out your room? Or what flavour crisps it likes best?"

"Oh, Ally! Don't be all sarky like Linn!" Rowan begged, which instantly made me drop the flip stuff. There's nothing like being compared to super-sensible (i.e. super-no-fun) Linn to make you yearn to be irresponsible and vaguely stupid.

"OK! OK, Ro! *Maybe* it'll work. What do we have to do?"

"Yay!" Rowan clapped her hands excitedly. "Right, first you have to sit like me..."

I tried to cross my legs, which on the floor would be quite easy, but in a blow-up green plastic chair is actually quite tricky (and wobbly). Then I held my arms out and rested my wrists on the sides of the chair, palms facing up.

"Next, you have to close your eyes, and

concentrate on being very still and emptying your head of all thoughts for a few minutes..."

Well, that shouldn't be too hard – I'd just spent most of the morning staring at lettuce leaves being eaten and thinking about absolutely nothing at all (except how bored I was).

So I closed my eyes and tried to concentrate on being very still. Only I became very *dizzy*, since I was concentrating so hard on being still that I'd forgotten to breathe.

Once I started breathing again, I couldn't concentrate on concentrating because of an irritating itch on my thigh, where the thread I'd pulled earlier on my shorts was tickling me. I didn't want to move my arm to scratch it in case that ruined everything, so I tried wriggling ever so slightly. And if you didn't know, wriggling bare skin against plastic makes surprisingly realistic farting noises.

I didn't dare open my eyes to see how much I was irritating Rowan. Instead, I tried being still again, which lasted quite a long time; at least five seconds, before my stomach – starved, after a minuscule breakfast of cornflakes, beans on toast and a packet of salt-and-vinegar crisps – started rumbling and creaking like an ancient wooden sailing ship at sea.

Five more seconds of relative quiet (after my

tummy died down) and I nearly jumped out of my skin as Rowan began talking in this low, *slowwww* voice that wasn't anything like her normal twitter.

"Hellooooo, Poltergeist! Arrre yoooooo *therrrrre?*"

I held my breath and waited.

Nothing.

Not a sound, not squelch not a tummy rumble.

"Pleeeaaaassse, oh Poltergeist! Give usss a *signnnn!*"

That time, there nearly *was* a noise – of me trying not to splutter out a giggle. Screwing up my face really tight, I struggled to keep it in, then just as I got the runaway giggle under control, I heard a Something. A *definite* faint tap-tapping Something.

And there – there was *another* Something; a deep reverberating noise, very close by. With my heart lurching halfway up my throat, I flipped my eyes open at the exact same moment as Rowan, and there – before us was ... Rolf, burping another reverberating dog-food scented burp, before settling himself down beside us for a serious bum-licking session.

Hmm. I could be wrong, but I think that kind of spoiled the mood and put paid to Rowan's spookalicious meditation stuff for today...

Chapter 8

SLEEPLESS AND SPOOKED

It was one of those really uncomfortable hot nights; you know – one of those where you feel as if your body's made of sticky-toffee pudding and it's totally impossible to sleep.

It was about 11.30 p.m. (possibly – my wonky, out-of-order bedside clock had finally given up telling even the *wrong* time and ground to a halt altogether) and I was sitting at my open window, trying to catch a wisp of a breeze on my face while staring off at Alexandra Palace in the distance, all lit up for some fancy function or other. I really wished I was there instead of here in my stuffy attic room, like an overheating Cinderella. (Unless, of course, it was the UK Undertakers' Annual Award Ceremony or the British Butchers' Oscars or something. Then I might not be *quite* so keen.)

A couple of thoughts were glooping around in my semi-melted mind, apart from fancy (or not) parties I was missing. What on earth were these spooky "ley-lines" that Billy had said were all around Ally Pally? I didn't want to ask him when he mentioned them on Sunday, because there's nothing more infuriating than Billy getting all excited 'cause *he* knows something *you* don't. Actually, when I dredged my memory banks, I remembered Mum once mentioning that Glastonbury Tor in Somerset – the hill Tor's named after – was built on ley-lines, or had ley-lines crossing it, or whatever ley-lines *do*, but I never bothered asking her at the time what that meant, and she wasn't exactly around to ask these days (in case you hadn't noticed). Maybe I'd check with Dad or Grandma tomorrow … on second thoughts, maybe *not* Grandma ("My, my! What a lot of hocus-pocus nonsense, Ally! Now what about giving me a hand relining these drawers...").

The other thing I was thinking about was whether I should try the "Totally, Utterly Charming Charm" again tonight, since it didn't look like I was about to fall into a deep, relaxing sleep any time soon. After all, I had bought a packet of nutmeg in the Turkish shop along the road – the only problem was that I'd have to sneak outside in the garden for the reinstated conch shell from Stanley's grave again, and even though I didn't *really* believe in this so-called poltergeist supposedly fluttering around our place, I wasn't a hundred per cent keen on wandering the house at midnight to prove to myself whether it existed or not. Apart from that, my best white knickers were worn and back in the laundry basket, so bang went another ingredient for the spell...

I'm well used to hearing my bedroom door open by itself in the night – mainly because it's *not* by itself; there's always a small, furry animal to blame, come up to keep me company overnight (and keep me awake with their snoring). What I'm *not* so used to is the door being flung open so wide that it clunks hard against the desk then wallops shut again.

"I heard the noises!" said a startled-looking Spiderman in the doorway, while I concentrated very, *very* hard on not having a heart attack.

"What – the tap-tapping thing?" I checked with Tor.

"*And* the scratch-scratching!" he added in a whisper as he darted towards my bed and dived straight under the duvet.

It was obvious how terrified he was – if Mr Penguin had been real, that bird would have been well and truly strangulated by the fierce grip Tor had on his neck.

"What's going on, Al? You woke me up!" blinked Linn, pushing the door open for the second time in the last half a millisecond and hovering in the darkened attic landing in a ghostly white night-dress, with her blondish hair tumbling loose and wavy around her shoulders.

I don't know what startled me more: the possibility that the poltergeist was up to its tricks again and tap-tapping around the place, or seeing Linn's hair curly and unstraightened for the first time in years. She hates those curls just as much as she hates being called Linnhe. Funny that, since both her real hair and real name are so pretty...

"Well?" she stared at me, then gazed more softly at the sight of Spiderman peeking out from under my covers. "Aw ... you haven't been hearing noises again, have you, Tor?"

"It's the tapping and scratching stuff," I explained, as Tor stared wordlessly at her.

"Hey ... you're not getting it into your head that it's ghosts, are you?" Linn smiled at him as she sat down on the edge of my bed.

"Maybe!" I felt like saying to her, but somehow I didn't think Linn would be as sympathetic to me as she was with our little brother.

Tor nodded a practically invisible nod in her direction.

"Well, let me tell you something – it's definitely *not* a ghost, right?" said Linn, in her finest impersonation of Grandma at her practical, no-nonsense best.

Tor didn't look convinced, and frankly, call me a wimp (you're a wimp, Ally Love!) but I wasn't exactly reassured either.

"And here's what we're going to do," Linn continued. "Me, you and Ally are going to go downstairs right now, sit in your bedroom and figure out where that noise is coming from. 'Cause once we find out what it is, then there won't be anything to be scared of, will there?"

Um, well, *maybe* – if we find out that it's a huge, towering poltergeist that's responsible for the racket...

Still, there was no real point trying to argue with Linn – even Tor knew that. So he slithered reluctantly out of my bed and took Linn's hand, holding his other hand (still clutching Mr Penguin) out to me. For his sake, I tried to be brave – which wasn't *too* hard since Linn was a) going first, and b) flicking the lights on as she went. And if I'd needed a reason c) well, it'd be the fact that if *I* was a poltergeist, *I'd* be pretty worried about coming face to face with my bossy sister.

"Look! Frankie and Derek are fast asleep down there!" Linn turned her head back and smiled at Tor, as we padded down to the first-floor landing.

"It's Fluffy and Eddie," mumbled Tor, deciphering the bundle of black-and-white fur intertwined in a snooze-ball at the foot of the attic steps, right beside the radiator.

"OK. Whoever," Linn whispered back, so we didn't wake Fluffy and Eddie (and Dad and Rowan, I guess). "But don't you see? If there was something up, the pets would be acting all weird, wouldn't they? And they're not!"

Speak about tempting fate; no sooner had Linn said those soothing words than Fluffy and Eddie woke up, their radar ears straining in the direction of the bedrooms, whirling around in search of some sound that we humans couldn't quite make out.

Yet.

Even though the lights were on, me, Linn and Tor nearly jumped out of our goosebumpy skin when Rowan's door flew open, and our wild-eyed, wild-haired sister came zooming out.

"Eek!" she squeaked, as startled to suddenly see us as we were to see her.

"What's wrong?" Linn barked at Rowan, trying to sound in control (though from where I was standing, she looked pretty shivery).

"Noises!" Ro hissed, pointing back towards her room. "I heard them!"

Before the summer holidays, we'd done *The Crucible* in English – that play about the Salem witches and whether or not all these ordinary village girls were *really* witches, or whether the whole village had gone a bit hysterical and hyped themselves into believing it. Well, maybe there *was* a pesky poltergeist swooping around our house, tapping on our walls and getting a good laugh at us panicking; or maybe we'd all gone a bit hysterical that night and hyped each other up. Who knows.

But what I *do* know is that Dad was very, *very* surprised to find his bed suddenly invaded by his entire family, two cats that weren't Colin and a furry toy penguin with a very squashed neck...

Chapter 9

THINGS THAT WENT "THUNK" IN THE NIGHT

Poltergeists or no poltergeists, when we all came charging into his room, I think Dad had been *most* alarmed by Rowan's hairdo.

She *did* look like one side of her head had come into contact with live electricity, but I think the reason it was sticking up like that had more to do with the way she'd been sleeping, before she'd been rudely awoken by the mystery noises.

Last night – aided by Rolf and Winslet, who thought he was playing some excellent game – Dad trawled the house for twenty minutes, looking and listening for the source of the strange tappings, scratching and now "thunking" sounds that both Tor and Rowan had heard.

"It was definitely more of a 'thunk'," Rowan had explained, huddled at the top of Dad's bed with Tor, while me and Linn scrunched ourselves under the duvet at the bottom of the bed, with blissfully purring cats that weren't Colin cuddled down between us all.

"Like a '*thunkity-thunk*'?" Tor quizzed Rowan.

"Um, *sort* of!" Ro nodded enthusiastically. "Did you hear that too?"

"Nope," Tor shook his head after a moment's thought.

Well, tap, scratch or thunk, Dad found no sign of anything normal or paranormal causing the noises. In fact the whole house seemed eerily silent…

"See? That's what you're all like at the moment!" Grandma sighed in exasperation this morning, when I tried to explain the strange goings-on in the middle of the night. "First, you say that hearing a noise is strange. *Then* you think *silence* is strange!"

Me and Rowan glanced at each other over the kitchen table and knew we'd goofed big-time by telling Grandma all. But then Tor had already told her most of it when she'd taken him round to his summer school craft class or whatever it was called. And since we were all yawning our heads off and had bags under our eyes from lack of sleep, she'd have suspected something was up anyway.

"Well, you know what *I* think."

Um, yeah, we *did* know what Grandma thought, but neither me or Rowan supposed she could resist telling us yet *again* that we were all getting far too over-imaginative and that all this ghost and spook stuff we'd been talking about recently was incredibly stupid for the following reasons:

1) Ghosts do not exist.

2) It wasn't good for any of us to go around believing they did, but it was *especially* not good for Tor to see his sisters taking it seriously.

3) There was a reasonable, rational excuse for everything that went "thunk" in the night.

Actually, if I'd been brave enough – or stupid enough – to argue that point with Grandma, I might have said that...

1) There was no way she could say for a fact that ghosts didn't exist. Well, she could *say* it, but it didn't mean that she was right.

2) We really didn't want to believe in them, or scare Tor. It was just that last night, we were. Scared, I mean. (Although Linn was trying to act all cool this morning and pretend she hadn't been *that* bothered. Ha! Well, who was that holding my hand under Dad's duvet last night, eh?)

3) If there was a reasonable, rational excuse for things that went thunk in the night, what was it? Aha – Grandma couldn't answer that, could she?

Dad's way of dealing with it last night was to come back to his room, tell us he'd drawn a blank, then spend the next half-hour telling terrible jokes till we were giggling enough to have shaken off the worst of our goosebumps and go back to bed. (Sample terrible joke: two elephants fall off a cliff – boom, boom!)

Grandma's way of taking our minds off all things spooksome today was to enlist me and Rowan in a top-to-bottom house-cleaning marathon. Or maybe she just planned on suctioning any rogue spirits into submission with the hoover.

"Well, I just think you all have too much time on your hands with these long summer holidays, that's the problem," Grandma carried on enlarging on her theory, whilst handing a can of polish and a duster to Rowan and a container of carpet freshener to me. "Keeping busy – that's the key. If you all keep busy, then your minds will be less likely to wander off with these silly fancies."

I was keeping my mind busy by shaking the word "poltergeist" on to the living-room rug with the carpet freshener (there was only enough room for "polterg-" unfortunately), when the door-bell rang.

"I'll get it!" I called upstairs to where Grandma and Rowan were helping kill off a bit more of the ozone layer by spraying polish over everything that didn't move.

"Hi..." Kyra yawned on my doorstep, looking for all the world like a girl who had a mind that was anything but busy. "God – this place smells ... clean!"

"Come in, why don't you," I said dryly, since Kyra was already halfway to the kitchen.

"Got any Coke?" she called over her shoulder, as she headed straight for the fridge.

"Maybe," I replied, following her in. "So what brings you round here?"

While she still had her back to me, I mouthed the words "Just ... *bored*" – at the exact same time as Kyra shrugged and mumbled, "Just ... *bored*," out loud.

That wasn't some spooky coincidence – that was just typical Kyra-speak. Kyra's natural state is bored. But she'd better be careful today – if Grandma got one whiff of her air of boredom she'd probably have Kyra scouring out the loo with a brush and a bottle of Mr Muscle before she got a chance to yawn again.

"Lilt! Excellent!" said Kyra, taking out a plastic bottle with a "Property of Linn Love!" Post-It note stuck to it. "Want some?"

(I couldn't exactly tell her to put it back, seeing as Rowan and I had a tendency to treat those Post-It notes of Linn's like they were invisible.)

"Yeah, OK," I replied, slopping myself down on to the nearest chair. "But you can't stay long – my gran's got this big clean-out planned and I'm supposed to be airing the mattresses or scrubbing the grouting or something next."

I hoped I'd got that right. Grandma reeled off such a list of chores earlier that I'd gone a bit giddy. For all I knew maybe she was expecting me to scrub the mattresses and air the grouting.

"Wow, *dull*." Kyra pulled a face as she yanked out a chair and sat down across from me with her drink. "So, any more of that weird stuff been happening again round here?"

"Too right! There was more clunking – or was it thunking? – going on last night and we all *freaked*. Me, Ro, Linn and Tor – we all ended up running into Dad's room, we were so scared!"

"Really!" Kyra's eyes flipped wide, looking a whole lot less bored now. "So you actually heard the ghost!"

"Well ... I didn't exactly *hear* it, but Rowan and Tor did!"

"Cool!" Kyra nodded slowly.

"*Alleeeee!* Who was that?" Grandma's voice drifted down from upstairs.

"Just Kyra!" I shouted back up to her, in case she was worried I'd answered the door to an axe-wielding maniac while she'd been polishing the bathroom taps.

"Oh, lovely. An extra pair of hands, then!" Grandma trilled back.

"Erm, no ... sorry, Mrs Miller – I can't stay!" Kyra called back, leaping to her feet and looking a lot more lively now that the threat of helping with housework loomed.

"So, maybe catch up with you tomorrow, then?" I asked her, as I followed her to the door, holding my hand out to take the glass she was still drinking out of.

"Well, of course!" Kyra frowned at me, as if I'd just said something incredibly dumb.

"What do you mean, 'of course'?" I frowned back at her.

An fleeting expression passed over Kyra's face – like the expressions little babies have when you don't know whether they're smiling at you or doing a poo in their nappy – and then something seemed to click into place in her mind.

"God, of course! I knew there was something I was meant to ask you! Two somethings, in fact!"

"What's that, then?"

Honestly, Kyra – what's she like? Her brain's like one big sieve. She goes to the bother of wandering round here then nearly leaves without asking me whatever she's supposed to want to ask me.

"Well, tomorrow … Sam's coming up to Crouch End to see me!" she beamed.

"Brilliant!" I smiled, genuinely pleased for her. "Are you excited?"

"Yeah, but a bit … y'know … *nervous*, too," she surprised me by saying.

It wasn't just the fact that the last thing I'd expect Kyra Davies to admit to was being nervous, but good grief; how can you spend a week snogging the face off some boy on holiday and then go all shy about seeing him? I don't think I'll ever understand the ins and outs of this dating thing. It's *way* too complicated for me. Fantasizing long-distance about Alfie gives me a twisty enough head as it is…

"Which is why I want you to come too, Ally."

"What?" I squeaked at Kyra, not sure I'd heard right.

"I just thought it wouldn't be so … y'know … *awkward*, if you were there, Ally."

For her and Sam maybe, but it would sure be awkward for me – specially if Kyra and Sam started playing tonsil tennis like they had every chance they got in Spain…

"Oh, and there was something else I meant to ask you – my mum's going to phone here tonight. My dad's on some course for work this weekend and Mum wants to go along with him for the sake of a free trip to a fancy hotel. So can I come and stay the weekend here? With you?"

What a girl – first she doesn't even have a reason for coming round here, then two seconds later she's hitting you with all these giant favours.

"I guess so…" I shrugged, pulling the front door open.

"Great!" said Kyra, walking backwards down the path towards the gate. "It'll be fun! I'll think up loads of stuff for us to do!"

Uh-oh…

"And I'll call you later once I know what time Sam's coming!"

Whoop-de-doo…

"Oh, and another thing, Ally," she grinned sheepishly from the other side of the garden gate now. "Can you bring Billy along? Just so Sam doesn't feel outnumbered by girls? 'Cause I thought if you pretended Billy was your boyfriend then…"

Whoah – maybe I was intrigued enough to meet the mighty Sam, and maybe friends are expected to do each other favours, but pretending Billy was my boyfriend? Wasn't that *way* beyond the call of duty…?

Chapter (10)

PHANTOM FISH...

"Ha, ha, ha, ha, ha!"

"Shut up, Billy."

"Ha, ha, ha, ha, ha, ha!"

"Look, it wasn't *my* idea to say you were my boyfriend, it was Kyra's, and I *told* her there was no way that was going to happen!"

"Ha, ha, ha, ha, ha!"

Honestly, I wished I'd never told Billy about Kyra's rubbish plan. I should have just asked him to come along with me to meet Sam with her tomorrow, simple as that. In fact, I wished I'd never phoned him about it at all. When I called earlier and spoke to his mum, I should have said it wasn't anything important and that he didn't have to call me back. But I didn't, and here I was now, having my eardrum blasted by his infuriating *braying*. Good grief, I was embarrassed enough about the notion of Sam thinking me and Billy were going out together when we met him tomorrow without Billy coming over like a donkey being told a dirty joke.

"You know, you don't *have* to come if you don't want to, Billy," I said sternly into the phone.

"Aw, don't be like that, Al!" said Billy, sobering up. "Course I'll come!"

"*Alleeee!* Your tea's getting cold!" Grandma shouted through from the kitchen.

"Listen, I've got to go," I told Billy. "But I'll meet you beside the Clocktower at eleven tomorrow morning, OK?"

"OK," Billy replied, sounding a lot more sensible. "Oh, and Ally –"

"What?"

"Should we hold hands when we see Sam?"

I cut off his snigger by shoving the phone down hard...

"What you got there, Tor?" I heard Grandma's boyfriend Stanley ask, when I walked back into the kitchen. Seemed like he was trying to suss out what the work of art was that was gracing our little brother's plate tonight.

Dad had gone out to his regular Wednesday night (spit, barf) line-dancing class, and Grandma had invited Stanley to have tea with us in an effort to keep us all "busy", I suspected, and less likely to spook ourselves silly as the night drew in, I guess. Just to keep the mood bright and breezy, I had a sneaking suspicion that she was going to make us play I-Spy or force us to sing rousing Scout songs or something once we'd finished eating. Or *not* eating, in Tor's case...

I know he always likes to turn his food into some kind of edible artwork before he gets stuck into it, but tonight Tor seemed to be more interested in staring down at the mound of beans he'd been working with (veggie burgers pushed uneaten to the side) than anything else.

"Tor?" Stanley prompted my brother again.

Linn leaned sideways to get a sneak preview of Tor's plate, and rolled her eyes. Tor spun it round for the rest of us to examine.

"Oh, right ... very good!" Stanley said feebly as he glimpsed the effigy of the beany goldfish swimming through a sea of mashed potato(?). Now even if the subject matter was a bit gloomy, I have to say the beans worked very well as individual orange fishy scales. But the mashed potato sea? What was all that about?

"Wouldn't you have been better using the noodles as waves?" our resident artist (Rowan) gently suggested. (What was this? A meal, or a masterclass in food sculpture?)

"Those are clouds," Tor corrected her, pointing at the white potato fluff with his fork. "It's Stanley in heaven..."

"Very nice, but now what about eating something?" Grandma said brusquely, leaning over and slapping one of his untouched veggie burgers into a bread roll and offering it to him on another plate.

Happily, Tor bit into that and Grandma took the opportunity to swoop all our plates away (including the effigy of Stanley Goldfish) and slap a giant, pastel-layered, whipped-cream-'n'-sprinkles-topped trifle down on the table between us. The thing is, Grandma always makes great food, but her puddings are usually a lot more sensible than this (cheesecake, home-made rice pudding, lemon meringue pie, that kind of thing). I don't know, but it seemed tonight like she was really overdoing the party atmosphere with this fancy trifle thing. That was it; she'd be getting out paper hats and streamers next and getting us to play Musical Chairs...

"So how's the summer job going, Linn?" asked Stanley, changing the subject and fulfilling his role tonight as cheery visitor (on Grandma's orders).

"Great! I served this woman today and you wouldn't *believe* how much she spent on her credit card. It was..."

As Linn talked, I was amazed by her transformation from last night; then, sitting curled up in Dad's bed, she was one of us, just as wild-eyed, wild-haired and spooked as me, Rowan and Tor (OK, maybe not as wild-haired as Ro). Today, she'd scraped back her blow-dried bob into a face-stretching ponytail and acted like last night had never happened. You know her problem? She just hates to lose her cool. I don't think she ever likes to seem vulnerable and scared. Hey, listen to me! I sound like I'm some proper, certified psychiatrist person (not bad, considering I only learnt to spell "psychiatrist" properly last year).

There was a moment of silence – apart from spoons clanging on pudding bowls – when Linn finally finished her story about the rich fat woman who blew a fortune on a tonne of clothes all a size too small for her. In that tiny silence, Tor gazed up from his still half-eaten burger (it'd take till midnight for him to finish his tea tonight, the way he was going) and spoke.

"The polterghost; do you think it's Stanley, come back to haunt us?"

At that moment, I stopped being scared of anything that went tap, scratch or thunk in the night and instantly gave up on the idea of a poltergeist being for real – the image in my head of a tiny ghostly goldfish paddling its way around the house was just *way* too funny. Poor Tor – none of us would have *ever* laughed deliberately at him, it's just that I don't think anyone could help themselves...

"Don't!" he pouted, gazing around a whole table of people choking with giggles.

"Ooh, Tor!" Grandma managed to say, wiping the tears from behind her glasses. "We didn't mean to! But listen, I told you before, there isn't any such thing as ghosts!"

"Your grandma's right!" Stanley backed her up quickly. "Everything's got a rational explanation, even if it takes a while to find out what it is. It's like the local paper trying to pretend that those gnomes up in Muswell Hill are moving on their own in the night. But mark my words, Tor, they'll soon find out who's really doing it!"

Unless it is something to do with that weird ley-line business, I thought to myself, remembering momentarily what Billy had said.

As Stanley spoke, Grandma poured the last of the milk into Tor's glass, but it was only half full. Automatically, she got up to go to the fridge for more.

"And anyway, there's certainly never been any reports of people seeing ghosts of fish!" Grandma smiled at Tor over her shoulder as she pulled the fridge door open. "In fact there's never been— Oh! How did that happen?"

We all stopped grinning and turned sharply in Grandma's direction. She was holding up a see-through plastic carton of milk, that was slowing turning from pure white to sea-green, as swirls of colour started twisting their way up from the bottom of the carton.

Uh-oh.

What was I saying about giving up on the idea of a poltergeist...?

Chapter 11

SECRETS AND BIG, FAT LIES

Once upon a time, long, long ago (Thursday lunchtime) there was a handsome prince from Wimbledon (stick with me here). He was as tall as the tallest tree (i.e. taller than me, Kyra, Sandie or Billy – I mean separately; not standing on each other's shoulders) with golden hair (i.e. blond) and eyes of deepest sapphire (i.e. blue). He was brave and strong and feared no one in the land (i.e. he was a right show-off and couldn't stop talking about himself).

And he chewed gum non-stop. Yuck.

"...and then when I scored the *third* goal – *chomp, chomp, chomp* – no one could believe it!"

"Three goals? Not bad!" Billy shrugged. He was sat at a table in our local KFC. "I scored four myself in my last match."

I felt Sandie nudge me in the side with her elbow. I knew what she meant – Billy was lying his baseball-capped head off.

"Yeah? So – *chomp, chomp, chomp* – the coach

says to me afterwards, 'Sam! You've *got* to be team captain again this year!' and I says, 'No, man – I want to stand down; I want to give someone else a break. I've been team captain for the last two years running!' An' he says, 'Yeah, but, Sam – you're the best player we've *ever* had!' So *I* says..."

"*I* was nearly team captain once," Billy tried to squeeze his way into the conversation with another downright lie. (When was Billy ever "nearly" captain of his football team? And since when had he scored four goals in a match for that matter? In his dreams, *that's* when...)

"Yeah, is that right?" Sam raised his eyebrows at Billy. "Anyway, like I was saying – *chomp, chomp, chomp* – I says to him, 'Listen, mate...'"

Sam sort of reminded me of someone, but I couldn't think who. Maybe if he shut up for five seconds I might be able to concentrate and remember.

"Gerroff!" I hissed at Billy, feeling his hand suddenly creep over mine.

I yanked my fingers away fast, immediately picking up the half-finished chicken burger on my plate, even though I hadn't been in the mood to eat any more up till then. (*Anything* to keep my hands out of Billy's clutches.)

Billy pulled a face, as if he was heartbroken at

my lack of lovey-doveyness. Good *grief*. He'd been doing this sort of stuff since the minute we met up with Sam and Kyra at the Clocktower on Crouch End Broadway. Trying to hold my hand; looking dreamily at me; calling me "babe" while I scowled at him...

You know, Billy might have been finding all this pretending-to-be-my-boyfriend business highly amusing (specially since I'd warned him *not* to do it) but I tell you something, as soon as I got him on his own he was dead *meat*. I mean, that's why I'd asked Sandie along at the last minute today too, just so it didn't look so much like me and Billy were an item. (Perish the thought...)

"...and then at the football-club disco I was DJing—"

"What a coincidence – *I've* done a bit of DJing too," Billy lied again.

"Yeah? Anyway – *chomp, chomp, chomp* – next thing, this guy comes up to me and says, 'You've got some wicked records, man – you should be on the radio!'"

"People have said that to me too!" Billy jumped in, fibbing his head off.

Sandie gave a little squeak of disbelief, that she quickly turned into a cough.

"Uh-huh," nodded Sam. "Anyhow, I says, 'Well,

I'd love to, mate, someday,' – *chomp, chomp, chomp* – and this fella says, 'Sorted! My mate's got a pirate radio station!'"

I kicked Billy under the table just as he was about to speak. I knew he was going to come out with "Hey, *I've* got a pirate radio station too!" or something just as monstrously ridiculous. And while I know Billy was only doing it for a laugh (like acting the loving boyfriend to me), I knew Sam hadn't spotted the sarcasm yet. And if he did, then he might not be too happy with Billy. And Kyra might not be too happy with Billy for spoiling her date. Not that she looked too impressed with her date right now, though. The thing is, Kyra has rotten taste in boys (I wouldn't touch any of the lads she likes with a specially extended bargepole), but as long as they a) are good-looking, and b) pay her a lot of attention, that'll please her. So far, Sam was doing fine as far as a) was concerned (he was definitely no ug), but was failing miserably when it came to b)...

"Anyway," Sam went on (and on, and on), "then this guy says – *chomp, chomp, chomp* – 'Honestly, one word from me and you'll be on there, mate! With your own show and everything!' So I gets his mate's phone number and next thing I call him and *he* says to me..."

There was just no shutting Sam up. It was as if he was a good-looking Furby fitted with batteries that never ran down. How he'd managed to eat his chicken nuggets and fries without pausing for breath I just don't know. He didn't even seem to need any of us to respond to him in any way, never mind chip in with a bit of conversation ourselves. I think that's why Billy was getting bored and entertaining himself by winding me up and taking the mick out of Sam without him noticing (yet).

Kyra, meanwhile, was sitting with her chin in her hands, her eyes gazing sideways (and glazing over) at Sam, a look of total boredom on her face. Poor Sam – I don't think he had the faintest idea that he was steadily talking himself out of a second date with Kyra. But then at this rate, how were the three of us going to escape from this *first* date? Were we destined to sit here till next week, as Sam reeled off all his many talents? When would he give us a chance to get a word in edgeways? That word being, "Bye!"...

"...he'd love to hear my stuff – *chomp, chomp, chomp* – and that what I should do is send him a demo tape..."

You know, the way Sam talked about all the amazing things he'd done, you'd think he was twenty-nine, not fourteen. Which made me kind of wonder if it wasn't just Billy that was coming out with the fiberoonies.

"...and it's like, if you get on pirate radio – *chomp, chomp, chomp* – then you *definitely* get spotted by proper stations, like Kiss FM and Radio One..."

Good grief, Kyra was actually yawning out loud – making a noise and everything – and *still* Sam droned on.

"...so, you know, maybe in a couple of years – *chomp, chomp, chomp* – I'll be famous!"

Suddenly, I realized who Sam reminded me of ... that big-headed cockiness, that whole me, me, me attitude – he was a dead ringer for Linn's old boyfriend Q (yes, Q: Q for Quite a plonker). But at least Kyra was smart enough to spot that straight away, unlike Linn, who swooned over Q for far too long and then got her heart well and truly squished. And it wasn't just Q, I realized suddenly – the way Sam was boring us to death with all his exploits and opinions, he wasn't too different from Keith "I've got a GCSE in Droning On" Brownlow, who I went out with for half a minute last year. (Half a minute too long...)

"Hey, I'm *already* famous!" Billy shrugged, as he came out with his latest big, fat lie.

"Oh yeah? How?" Sam grinned at Billy disbelievingly.

Wow – Billy had managed the impossible; Sam had actually asked someone else a question for once (in his life?). I couldn't wait to hear what inventive story was going to trip out of Billy's mouth now. Probably something about being Madonna's secret love child or holding the world record for juggling aardvarks or something.

"Check this out!" Billy grinned, leaning across to the next table and grabbing some raggedy, already-read newspaper lying there.

He held it up so it was facing Sam and Kyra, which meant me and Sandie had to lunge across the table (with me getting tomato sauce smeared on my T-shirt for my trouble) and twist our heads around to see what was so interesting.

"*The Hornsey Journal*. 'Parking Charges Cause Outrage'. Um, Billy – what are we supposed to be looking at exactly?" Kyra frowned.

"No, not that – *that!*"

Billy tapped some story further down on the front page.

"'Gnome From Gnome – the mystery of the Muswell Hill Gnomes continues, with more of the little men marching into other gardens in the middle of the night.'" I read aloud, straining my neck around to see the feature, and the accompanying photo of a gnome up a tree and a very disgruntled looking old man pointing up at it.

"So?" Kyra shrugged, practically doing an Elvis impersonation with her lip curled up like that.

"So, that's me!" grinned Billy. "Me and Steven and Hassan! *We're* the ones moving the gnomes and stuff around!"

Now Sandie really *did* squeak, and was too surprised even to cover it up with a cough this time.

"You're kidding?!" beamed Sam, suddenly genuinely interested in what someone else had to say (amazingly).

"Nope," Billy shook his head – a proud smile splattered all over his face. "I'm not kidding. It's all down to us!"

"So it's *you* that's been driving all those boring old farts demented!" Kyra laughed out loud, grabbing the paper for a closer look.

"Guilty!" said Billy. "We were only going to do it the once, but then it got in the papers last week, and that was such a total buzz that we—"

"Um, Billy?" I interrupted him, feeling a bit like I'd been slapped around the head with a large fish I was so confused. "Is this another lie?"

Well, I had to ask, since everything *else* he'd

been blabbering on about for the last hour or so had all been wildly untrue.

"Nope – it's for real," he shook his head. "Cross my heart and hope to die."

"But you ... you were talking about it on Sunday when we met up," I pointed out to him. "And you never admitted that it was you!"

"I know! What a laugh, eh?" Billy beamed.

"And when exactly were you planning on telling me?" I demanded, feeling weirdly let down. Me and Billy *never* had secrets from each other – ever. It had been that way since we first knew each other, and the first secret I remember him blabbing to me was that he'd just done a wee in the paddling pool we were both splashing about in (don't worry – this wasn't last year or anything; we were only three years old at the time).

"Dunno!" Billy answered dumbly, like the big, lanky, annoying, gnome-meddling goofball he can sometimes be.

I guess that Billy's confession had made me feel weird for another reason: now that I knew the mystery of the gnomes was man-made (make that *boy*-made) instead of something supernatural, where did that leave all the weirdness back home?

A sample of the questions sloshing around my head:

Just what exactly was responsible for the milk in our fridge turning green last night?

Was it all down to ghastly ghostliness?

Or what?

And what could we expect next?

Eggs that turned tartan when you cracked them in the frying pan...?

Urgh. *Everything* was getting so confusing that it was melting the few brain cells I have in my head...

Chapter 12

YOU ARE FEELING VERY SLEEPY...

Sam was history.

I think he thought that me, Sandie and Billy going with him and Kyra on the bus down to Finsbury Park tube station was a sign that we really liked him, but how wrong could a boy be? The real reason was that when he'd nipped to the loo in KFC (a blissful few minutes without him yakking on) Kyra had *begged* us all not to leave her alone with Sam, in case she fainted with boredom or something.

Anyway, Sam sure got the message when he was saying his goodbyes and told Kyra he'd call her. In reply to that, Kyra just shrugged and said, "Whatever," while staring at a point somewhere over his shoulder. If he *didn't* get the message then, he sure did when he leant over to kiss her and she ducked sideways so that he ended up smooching thin air.

Good grief, it was all so pointed and embarrassing that I didn't know where to look. Billy, of course, hugely enjoyed watching every moment of Sam's mortification, leaning himself back on the tube station railings and happily clocking the goings-on as if he was watching an episode of *The Simpsons*.

"What I want to know is," Billy quizzed Kyra, when we were hanging out in the actual park at Finsbury Park after we'd got shot of Sam, "how come you never noticed he was so boring when you were on holiday?"

"Guess I was too busy snogging him," Kyra shrugged casually.

"Kyra!" Sandie gasped at our friend's total lack of shame.

"Ah, come on, Sandie!" Billy sniggered. "Don't you get a joke when you hear one?"

Sandie pursed her lips and stared daggers at Billy, who just carried on sniggering at Kyra's funny comment till he noticed by her stony face that Kyra *hadn't* been joking after all; she actually *meant* what she'd just said.

Hmm ... in my short snogging history (one very duff kiss off Keith Brownlow in the dim and distant past) I'd come to the conclusion that it is always better to *like* someone before you get around to the snogging part, otherwise it feels pretty creepy to realize afterwards that you've locked lips with a total creep/dweeb/loser/bore/whatever.

And what had just gone on with Kyra and Sam made me even *more* certain of that fact. Still, it wasn't as if I had a queue of creeps/dweebs/losers/bores/whatever desperate to kiss me anyway, so I guess I didn't exactly have that dilemma to worry about any time soon.

"Hey, Ally, it looks like your gran is running a crèche out there!"

The four of us had just arrived back at my house after we'd got bored of mooching around Finsbury Park, and Kyra was squinting out of the kitchen window at the collection of kids currently pootling around on our daisy-splattered, slightly overgrown lawn, while Grandma sat flicking through a copy of *Hello* magazine with one hand and switched the radio by her side off and on with a finger on her other hand. It looked like the kids were playing a version of Musical Chairs, only with cushions scattered on the ground. At this precise moment though, the game was lurching towards confusion, seeing as a cat that wasn't Colin had settled down on one of the cushions for a snooze, while Winslet had just made a grab for another of the cushions and was now running behind the shed with it. Meanwhile, Grandma was too engrossed with someone famous's stylishly designed kitchen to notice what was going on and act as referee/cat-shooer/cushion-rescuer.

"They must be some of Tor's buddies from that summer club thing he's been going to," I told Kyra and the others, as I stared out at a bunch of kids I didn't recognize. Apart from one; Amir the refugee kid was easy to spot – the look of serious bewilderment on his face gave him away. Obviously he hadn't a clue what Musical Cushions was all about and was trying to figure out why the old lady kept switching the radio off and whether chasing dogs was part of the rules or not.

"Can I get a juice or something…"

I was about to tell Billy that sure, he could help himself to whatever was in our fridge, when he went and said something *really* dumb.

"…darling?" he added with a face-splitting grin.

"Call me 'darling' once more and I won't let you come back here," I warned Billy, pushing past him and grabbing a carton of already opened orange off the worktop and three glasses out of the kitchen cupboard (one glass for me, one glass for Kyra, one glass for Sandie and *no* glass for Mr Joker).

"Aww, please!" Billy whimpered pathetically, following me and the girls as we ambled out of the back door into the sunshine. "I'm thirsty!"

"Ignore him," Sandie muttered to me, obviously enjoying this game of winding Billy up.

"Don't worry, I will. Hi, Grandma!" I called out,

ignoring Billy entirely as I flopped down on the grass.

"Hello, dears!" Grandma smiled over, lifting her gaze from the magazine pages, and then noticing with a start the chaos going on all around her.

"Please, please, pretty please," Billy whimpered some more, holding out an old, empty jam jar he must have grabbed from somewhere or other.

"Billy, if you promise to quit the boyfriend gags, you can have as much juice as you want!" I told him sternly.

Even after we'd said a not-very-fond farewell to Sam, Billy had kept up a steady stream of silliness all afternoon, involving calling me "Snookums" really loudly when a bunch of young mums were passing in the park and embarrassing me stupid by falling to his knees and pretending to propose to me on the top deck of the W3 bus.

"I promise, Ally, I promise! No more boyfriend gags!"

I saw Sandie roll her eyes, knowing as well as I did that Billy was about as likely to stop fooling around as I was to get a Nobel prize for Braininess in Maths. But what could I do? Billy had the sort of soulful expression on his face that Rolf uses when he's sitting beside you trying to guilt-trip you into giving him the last sausage on your plate.

"OK," I gave in, pouring orange into the jam jar Billy was holding out with both hands, Oliver Twist style. "Where did you get that anyway?"

"It was on the window sill," Billy explained, before he glugged down practically the whole of his jar full of juice in one gulp.

I was going to mention that it was probably highly unhygienic to drink out of a dusty jam jar but I did once witness Billy knocking back Coke out of his trainer for a dare, so I didn't suppose a light dusting of dust particles was going to do much harm to his already mistreated stomach.

"Ally, dear," Grandma's voice suddenly loomed close. "Can you keep an eye on this lot while I go in and get them some nibbles?"

"Sure," I replied dubiously, wondering why Grandma thought Tor and his mates needed supervising. None of them were particularly little; it wasn't as if they were at the stage of eating earth or sticking stones up their noses.

"I caught that blond-haired boy trying to drag the hedge cutter out of the shed to play with earlier, and the girl with the plaits goes hysterical when she sees a bee," Grandma explained the situation without me having to ask her out loud.

I guess it was a good idea to watch this lot after all – our family wouldn't be too popular with a few parents if their kids came home looking like they'd been blood-soaked extras in *Scream*. Speaking of screams, I was glad Grandma warned me about the plait-girl. As long as I knew any yelping from her was to do with small flying bugs, I wouldn't panic that she'd just clapped eyes on our resident poltergeist...

"So anyway," Kyra began talking as soon as Grandma had disappeared into the kitchen, "I was thinking about fun things to do when I stay over this weekend."

God – I'd forgotten about that. I had the dubious privilege of Kyra's company for three whole nights (and days), starting from tomorrow. The very thought of it made me tired already.

"And I thought that tomorrow night, maybe we should have a sleepover with all the girls – out here in the garden!"

"Oh, yes!" sighed Sandie.

"What – in tents?" Billy asked, pretty densely. I mean, what did he expect us to sleep in? Cardboard boxes? Egg cartons?

"*Yes*, in *tents*," Kyra droned sarkily at him.

"I'd have to check with my dad that it's OK," I told her, though I knew Dad would be fine with it (he just likes to be asked, that's all).

"Cool! Well, if you ask him tonight, then we

could phone all the other girls and get it sorted!"

"What about the boys?" Billy frowned at Kyra.

(Out of the corner of my eye, I could see the girl with the plaits sidling over to us. Maybe she thought that she'd be safer with us; that bees were allergic to teenagers or something.)

"What about *what* boys?" Kyra frowned back at him.

"Well ... *me*! Can *I* be part of the sleepover?" Billy asked pleadingly. "I'll bring my own tent!"

I could tell without looking that Sandie was now pulling a face – she could only stand short bursts of time exposed to Billy, and a whole night of him mucking around would be filling her with dread right now. But me and Kyra, well, we stared at each other dubiously, deliberately teasing Billy. I mean, *I* knew that *she* knew that we both thought that sounded like fun, but it was also fun to torment Billy into thinking we'd say no for a moment or two.

"No *way*!" I shook my head at him.

Billy looked crestfallen, like I'd just told him I'd sold his PlayStation 2 for £1.50 to a passing stranger.

"I mean, no *way* would we have an outdoor sleepover without you!" I giggled at him.

"Aw, brilliant!" he sighed with relief. (You know,

sometimes it's just *too* easy to take the mickey out of Billy...)

"That jar thing," said a small high-pitched voice beside us, as Billy took a final swig of orange juice.

"What about it?" I asked plait-girl, wondering why she was so interested in what Billy was drinking out of. OK, so it wasn't exactly a normal glass, but it wasn't exactly an Adidas trainer either.

"Sanjeev was using it to carry worms around in."

Billy coughed and spluttered for quite a long time after that. Sandie tried patting him on the back (which was pretty public-spirited of her, considering they don't get on), but all that did was make him shoot orange juice straight out of his nose. (Plait-girl was pretty fascinated by that particular trick.)

Speaking of tricks...

"Um, Ally, what exactly is your brother doing?" Kyra asked me, dragging my attention away from Billy and his exploding nostrils.

At first glance, I had no idea what my brother was doing – all I could see was a semicircle of kids grouped around Tor. I rose up on to my knees for a better look, and spotted that Tor was very slowly drawing a line with a piece of chalk along the paving stones of the garden path, and that Britney (our semi-pet pigeon) was trotting along, eyes transfixed by the ever-growing white chalk line.

"Oh, he's hypnotizing the pigeon!" I explained to Kyra, as if hypnotizing pigeons was the most normal thing in the world.

"*Excuse* me?" said Kyra, staring at me as if I'd just announced that Radio One was going to replace their Top Twenty playlist with 24-hour monk chanting.

"There was this animal programme on the other night," I tried to explain a little more clearly. "This guy in America, he did the chalk line trick with a chicken, and it seemed totally hypnotized; it just stared and stared at this line he was drawing. Tor's obviously giving it a go."

I don't know if Kyra was too impressed, but all Tor's buddies were, even if they came across slightly on the scared side too. Especially poor bemused Amir, who probably didn't know what to expect next.

"Hi, guys!" Rowan's voice called out from the kitchen doorway, as she stepped out into the garden with a tray piled high with buns and plates that Grandma must have sent her out with. "Come and get it!"

I don't know for sure, of course, but from the way Amir reacted, I think he thought "Come and get it!" meant "I am an evil witch and I'm going to eat all of you children, starting with that little Afghan kid that doesn't speak English!"

Rowan – looking even more goth today than she had at Stanley the goldfish's funeral – looked on, confused, as a whole bunch of small people went berserk, following Amir's lead and screaming their heads off.

"Polterghost!" yelled plait-girl, pointing at my sister before diving behind Billy for protection.

I guess I didn't really have any thoughts about what a poltergeist would look like if it materialized, but I didn't really think it would resemble a fifteen-year-old girl in a long, black cotton dress, with millions of bangles on her arms, red lipstick, too much black kohl eye pencil and a big, back-combed hairdo. But according to Tor's summer club class mates, that's *exactly* what a "polterghost" looked liked.

"Wahhhh! Make the ghost go away!" squealed someone inconsolable, as Britney snapped out of her trance and fluttered, panic-stricken, into her favourite tree.

"Tor!" Grandma's voice bellowed out above the mayhem. "What *exactly* have you been telling your friends?"

Tor bit his lip and went white.

Hmm ... suddenly he was a *lot* more worried about getting into trouble from our disapproving gran than the spook he'd been boasting to his friends about...

Chapter 13

SPOOKINESS AND SARCASM

You'd think Kyra had already come to stay, the way she'd hung around all day after the Sam boreathon and the business of Rowan being mistaken for something supernatural (instead of just something super-airhead).

And she wasn't the only one – Sandie and Billy didn't seem in any hurry to scoot homewards either.

When Grandma said, "You're all welcome to stay for tea, dears…", Kyra, Sandie and Billy had answered yes before Grandma had even had a chance to finish the rest of her sentence, which was "…but I'm sure your parents are expecting you home." Then, as soon as the macaroni and cheese was eaten and Grandma and Dad had left (Grandma for her flat and a cosy night in with Stanley, and Dad for a drink to celebrate some buddy's birthday), Kyra was straight on the phone, checking with the rest of our friends that they were all up for tomorrow's outdoor sleepover.

After that, she took turns with Sandie and Billy using the phone to call their folks and ask if it was OK to hang around and watch a movie at ours tonight.

Talk about making yourself at home...

"*BOO!*" Billy roared over the back of the sofa, directly in Sandie's ear.

"Billy!" I barked at him, since Sandie was so shocked she'd temporarily lost the ability to *breathe*, never mind speak.

"Are you trying to give me a heart attack?" Rowan turned and asked him, while Billy just grinned broadly and went round to take his place – sprawled on the beanbag.

"Did I miss anything?" he asked, staring at the TV.

"Nope. I mean, is this guy *seriously* meant to be scary?" Kyra snorted at the drooling werewolf lunging at the young girl on the screen.

"Um, *yeah*," I nodded at her, from behind the safety of a cushion.

At least I wasn't the *only* one being a wuss. From the glazed look of terror in Sandie's eyes (it was there *before* Billy tried to frighten her to death), I think she was regretting staying to watch this movie and was wishing she was at home with her mum and dad watching nature documentaries about the migratory habits of wombats or the mating rituals of slugs or whatever on the Discovery Channel. Good grief, she was even holding hands (make that *gripping* hands) with Rowan on the sofa right now.

And, it has to be said, it was a bit of a joke that Rowan looked so equally gobsmacked with fear at this video, since *she* was the one who brought it home today, on loan from her mate Chazza. "He says it's really amazing!" she'd twittered, when she'd fished it out of her bag. Amazingly *terrifying*, more like. I knew I'd have nightmares about it tonight (just as well Tor was safely tucked up in bed with his many soft toys and a live cat or two), and I could bet Rowan and Sandie would be tripping down nightmare avenue later as well (Billy too, but he'd never admit to it). Hard-nosed Kyra, on the other hand, would probably dream happy dreams of yawning in the face of ex-boyfriends who bored her...

"Where'd you say your dad was going tonight?" Kyra turned to me and asked conversationally, while reaching over to the bowl of tortilla chips on the table and tickling Rolf's tummy on the way there.

Honestly, Kyra was acting so casual and

uninterested that you wouldn't think someone was being gnawed to death by a guy in a furry suit and bulging eyes on the telly.

"Told you," I muttered, wincing at the blood spurting in copious amounts. "He's gone out with some people from his Wednesday line-dancing class."

Kyra snorted so loudly at the reminder of my dad's embarrassing hobby that Rolf, Rowan and Sandie jumped in surprise and/or shock. (It didn't seem to register with Billy, who was now engrossed in the movie while picking his nose.)

"Oh, come on!" Kyra frowned at my sister and best friend, cowering together on the sofa. "Why are you two so jumpy? It's only a dumb film! It's all just fake blood and tomato sauce! And those aren't *real* intestines!"

"Actually," Billy suddenly veered back into the conversation again, "I think they *are* real, but they're not human, they're just *cow* intestines or something."

As Rowan started to whimper (while Sandie made a weird gagging noise), I thought it was perhaps as good a time as any to scarper to the kitchen for Coke and tortilla-chip refills.

Only *I* was the one jumping with surprise and/or shock when I saw what was in the kitchen...

"Uh, hi, Ally!" Alfie drawled, sitting on a chair with his jeaned legs and best Van trainers draped across the kitchen table.

Wow, he was looking spectacularly beautiful tonight. His naturally fair/blond hair had just been cut to a spiky crop, and I think (but couldn't be sure, since the main light was off and only the raggedy table lamp squished in by the bread bin was throwing out some low-level light) that he'd had his hair bleached even lighter. Grandma wouldn't approve of that (she hates anything fake, from hair-dye to tattoos to boob jobs to smarmy TV presenters), but *ooh* I thought Alfie looked particularly gorgeous. Even though I hadn't a clue why he was unexpectedly sitting here in my low-lit kitchen, radiating gorgeousness and – get this – staring at me with this beatific smile.

(Beatific: what an amazing word. I just learned it the other day in English class. It means "displaying great happiness" or "having a divine aura". Basically, think of that super-happy, blissed-out expression the Mona Lisa has in that mega-famous painting by Leonardo da Vinci. That's the expression Alfie had on his face now, and – omigod – he was looking straight at me!)

"Um, so what are you doing here anyway?" I asked Alfie, hoping he was about to fall to the floor and declare undying love and devotion. To *me*, I mean.

(Hey, who needed spooky spells with silly ingredients done at inhospitable times of the night? Alfie was staring at me like a handsome, blond, spiky boy version of the Mona Lisa. Like I was some desirable thirteen-year-old, messy-haired, trainer-and-jean-loving goddess. Magic? I didn't need magic when Alfie was smiling at me like he was…)

"I was just waiting for Linn. She's upstairs getting changed. Then we're going out to a mate's party."

I waited for him to add, "But of course, that's all a lie – I'm really using that as an excuse to hang out here with you, Ally!" But strangely, Alfie didn't say that out loud. Then again, my hopes weren't *completely* dashed; he was still doing that beatific staring in my direction. Except, when I moved towards the bag of tortilla chips by the bread bin, I noticed that Alfie's beatific expression didn't move when *I* did; instead it stayed fixed to the wall behind me.

"What?" I heard my slightly irked self say out loud.

"Oh!" Alfie laughed, and shook his head till he spun his gaze around to meet mine. "I was just checking out that thing on the noticeboard!"

I spun round to check out the "thing" that had held Alfie's attention so beatifically, or whatever fancy word you want to use.

And then I stopped dead. Now I saw what Alfie's expression *really* was; it wasn't "radiating happiness" or "divine", he was just smirking. Smirking at the torn-out page from a book that was pinned to our cork noticeboard.

Good grief – it was the "Totally, Utterly Charming Charm". How had it got there? Who – or should I say *what* – had sneaked into my room, ripped that out of the book I'd so carefully hidden and stuck it up here in the kitchen for all to see? I wasn't entirely sure what it felt like to have your blood run cold, but I sure was getting the oddest, shivery sensation zapping all over my body.

"One of Rowan's things, is it?" Alfie grinned at me, assuming that anything as frivolous as a love spell would have to be something to do with Love Child No. 2.

"Uh-huh," Love Child No. 3 (i.e. me) nodded, meanly letting Rowan take the blame for something Alfie obviously found so amusingly silly.

Or maybe it was just that I was so stunned to see it pinned there that my brain couldn't come up with anything else to say. (OK, so it was a little bit of both. Shock *and* meanness.)

"So, uh, what are you guys watching through there?" Alfie asked blithely, unaware of the weirdness of the situation.

"Um, some horror film..." I shrugged.

"Cool – I'll come and watch it for a bit," Alfie said, thumping his legs off the table and on to the floor. "I'm getting kind of bored waiting for Linn."

Tearing the love spell from the noticeboard and grabbing the bag of tortilla chips (while conveniently forgetting about the Coke – I was too spooked to be left in the kitchen on my own), I hurried after Alfie, fear mingling with excitement about where exactly he would sit to watch the movie. I mean, there was a beanbag leaning right up beside the armchair I'd been curled up in. If Alfie flopped himself down on to it, my hand would be within stroking distance of his spiky hair...

"Oh, hi, Alfie!" Rowan smiled at him as we walked into the living room. "Here, I'll budge up."

And with that one offer of budging up, all my hopes were dashed. Sandie and Kyra both threw me knowing looks (knowing, like they did, that my heart belonged to Alfie) as he settled himself down next to my sister on the sofa. My sister who had ditched the goth look, I noticed, after the business with the screaming kids earlier this afternoon.

Tonight she was back to more normal Rowan wear – clashing bright colours with a sunshiney sun-flower hairband holding her ponytail in place. No way were any small kids going to mistake her for a witch or a ghoul now. Someone who should be arrested by the fashion police, maybe, but definitely not an evil spirit. (Well, when have you ever seen an evil spirit in a butterfly T-shirt, candy-stripe trousers and furry pink pig slippers?)

"Is this any good then?" Alfie asked no one in particular.

"S'not bad," Billy shrugged in reply, absent-mindedly picking his stupid nose again while he goggled at the telly.

"Uh-huh." I watched Alfie shrug back. "So what's the plot?"

"Plot? Who needs a plot when you've got gallons of blood, guts and screaming?" came Linn's sarcastic answer from the doorway behind us.

I turned and peered at Linn, wondering what exactly had taken her so long. She'd arrived home from work a couple of hours ago wearing a fitted white T-shirt and black trousers, and she appeared to have changed into ... *another* white fitted T-shirt and different black trousers. Was it really worth the bother?

"Yeah, I know you don't like horror movies

much, Linn," Alfie spun his head around to answer her, "but some of them are really good! It's, like, all about atmosphere, isn't it?"

"Atmosphere?" Linn snorted, as some girl ran panting and panicking through darkened woods, the werewolf in hot pursuit. "All those filmmakers do is shoot the movie in the dark! That's not atmosphere – that's just saving lots of money on lighting bills!"

Maybe Linn thought her cynicism was cuttingly funny, but like the rest of us, I don't think she was laughing too much when all the lights in our house chose that exact moment to go out...

"What's going on?" Sandie squeaked from the far end of the sofa.

"Power cut! It has to be!" Linn announced assuredly.

"Oh, *yeah*?" said Kyra, that other Queen of Sarcasm. "Then how come the TV's still on?"

Sure enough, our house might have been plunged into darkness, but on screen, the terrifying werewolf was pouncing on his latest, screaming victim.

Oh, why hadn't Rowan brought home the latest Disney movie to watch tonight instead...?

Chapter 14

HUMAN JELLY

It wasn't the lights going out that woke Tor up
(he'd been happily sleeping in the dark for the last
half-hour, after all).

Oh, no – what got him scurrying down the stairs
in a panic was all the howling going on. Linn had
tried to shush the dogs, but you couldn't really
blame Winslet and Rolf for joining in once Rowan,
Sandie and Kyra had started the howling going in
the first place. (You could tell Billy was scared rigid
too, since he was totally – and unusually – silent.)

"Ally! Hurry up, *please*!" Kyra whined now.

If my hands weren't shaking so much, I *might*
have been able to hurry up, but as it was I was
finding it pretty difficult to get the match in my
quivering fingers to wobble anywhere near the big,
fat candles on our mantelpiece.

"Ally! Come *on*!"

And if my hands weren't shaking so much, I
might have been tempted to wrap them round
Kyra's neck and get her to shut up for a minute.

You know, it's funny how Kyra acts all confident and cocky, but two seconds after she'd answered back to Linn about the TV still being on, she'd bolted from the armchair and joined a whimpering Sandie and Rowan on the sofa. I mean, I was scared too, but at least I was trying to do something more useful than just join in the group howling. At least I'd found the matches and was attempting to get some light in the room, and I'd had the presence of mind to turn the video off and flip the telly on to *Brookside*, which was at least a little more comforting and normal than werewolves snacking on teenagers.

"Ally! What's *taking* you so long? Why don't you just light them?"

I flipped round to frown at Kyra's impatience, but by the glow of the TV screen and the one candle I'd managed to light so far, all I could make out was one quivering, mass of girl (and small boy) all intertwined and shivering on the sofa. From the snuffling and purring sounds I could hear, it seemed like Rolf and one or more cats were piled up on the sofa too, not because they were scared but because in the cat(s') case, it was a warm place to be – with so much body heat being generated in one place – and in Rolf's case, because it was a good game. Apart from that, there were two shadowy blobs on the floor; one was a beanbag and one was Billy.

"I just went next door!" Linn's voice called out from the hallway. "Michael and Harry's lights are all on, so it's not some weird kind of power cut!"

"And I just tried the upstairs lights," Alfie's voice called down from somewhere on high, accompanied by his muffled footsteps thudding on the stairs. "They're all working, so it's just the downstairs lights and the hall that are out!"

Wow ... that's strange, I thought, as I steadied my hand enough to light another couple of candles. *Why would a poltergeist just zap the downstairs lights? Why not go for the full fear factor and switch the whole house off?*

"Yeah, well, Michael said it was probably a fuse," Linn's voice drifted closer, as she walked along the hallway. "He's looking out some fuses for us now. But I think I'll run round and get Dad anyway; he's only in the pub up the road."

"I'll go if you want!" Billy called out suddenly, sounding extra brave. Or did he just want an excuse to get out of our ghost-riddled house?

"Don't go!" Sandie surprised everyone by squeaking in Billy's direction. Wow – she really must have had her brain scrambled by fear if she thought Billy could somehow protect us all from the heebie-jeebies.

"Thanks, Billy, but it's OK – I'll go," announced Linn, walking into the living room. "You could never pass as eighteen to get into the pub. And anyway, you'd probably be better staying here, and … I dunno … keeping everyone's spirits up or something."

"Um, OK," I heard Billy mumble dubiously.

"And while I'm out, Rowan," Linn continued, "could you…?"

Linn's sentence trailed off as she noticed the human jelly shivering on the sofa.

"Never mind," she said sharply, turning her attention from Rowan and Co and staring at me instead. "Ally, could you give Alfie a hand? The fuse box is in the cupboard under the stairs and he can maybe find the one we need to replace if you hold the torch for him."

I was vaguely aware of what Linn had just said, but I was particularly fond of the bit about me helping Alfie. And helping Alfie in a small cupboard sounded pretty good too.

"Sure!" I shrugged easily, and bolted for the door before Linn changed the plans.

"Um … anyone heard the one about th-the guy who goes into a pub with a fish under his arm?"

I heard Billy blabber, in his new role as chief cheerer-upper, as commanded by Linn.

But I didn't hang around to hear what happened to the guy, *or* his fish – I had my own important orders to carry out. Not that helping Alfie at close quarters was exactly a chore…

Out in the hallway, the glow of the streetlight outside poured through the opened front door. There was some brightness illuminating the first-floor landing too, 'cause of Alfie flipping on all the bedroom lights. Luckily for me, none of that light was in the right place to light up the cupboard under the stairs, so I took the torch Linn was holding out to me and sneaked myself in beside Alfie.

"Could you, uh, point it up there, do you think, Ally?" he asked me, blinking as I shone the beam directly in his beautiful face.

"Oh, sorry!" I apologized, angling the beam upwards, so all I could make out of Alfie was his angular hand reaching up with a screwdriver towards the fuse box. Round his wrist was tied the soft leather strips that he always wore. I suddenly felt as if all my senses were heightened; like I could smell things more sharply (and I don't mean just the stuffy dust in this cupboard). Alfie's hand wasn't close, but I was sure I could make out the scent of that worn leather bracelet of his. And that was *definitely* a whiff of hair wax or gel or whatever it was that he used to make his spiky hair spiky.

Just as I was doing this amazing impersonation of a police sniffer dog, I got a huge shock – and I wasn't the only one.

"What the hell was that?" Alfie panted in the dark, now that whatever furry thing was on top of us had knocked the torch out of my hand.

My heart was thundering so hard that it took me a moment to answer him. Then my super-heightened senses kicked in and I recognized the rough, non-animal furriness that was brushing my cheek.

"It's just Dad's old parka!" I exclaimed. "He hangs it up on a hook in here!"

I heard Alfie sigh a relieved sigh. Correction: I *felt* Alfie sigh a relieved sigh. And not just the air blowing out on my face, but his chest deflating where it was pressed against mine...

"What's wrong?" Linn's voice cut into the moment, as Alfie and I dropped our arms from around each other and sprang apart.

"I– I thought you'd, like, gone!" Alfie mumbled.

"Thought I'd better change into my trainers – it would have been too hard to run in these heels," Linn answered, pointing down with one hand to feet we couldn't see in the half-light.

As my sister glowered in the doorway of the cupboard, her face spookily lit by the beam of the torch I was wobbling around, I silently thanked the god of blown fuses or our resident poltergeist or whoever was responsible for letting me accidentally end up in Alfie's arms.

Maybe we'd only grabbed each other out of fear and maybe it had only lasted two seconds, but it was my first ever hug from Alfie and I'd never, *ever* forget it...

Chapter 15

NORMALLY NORMAL

Alfie did an excellent job of acting normal last night (i.e. ignoring me), after the cupboard incident.

He told Linn he didn't know enough about fuse boxes to go meddling in one, and helped out by leaving me (and the cupboard) behind and taking over my candle-lighting duties instead.

It's pathetic, I know, considering we'd all been scared witless by the spookiness of the situation, but I found myself swept away by the romantic glow of the candles. Or maybe it was just because I had my eyes firmly fixed on Alfie wandering about in the candlelight...

As soon as he'd lit enough – as well as the gorgeous antique gas lamps that Michael and Harry brought through from their house for us – Sandie and Kyra untangled themselves from Rowan, Tor and each other and scarpered home to their own, brightly lit, spook-free houses (as did Billy), so I didn't even get a chance to tell my girlie mates about my (accidental) hug with Alfie.

I'd love to have let them in on that blissful secret, but one person I *was* glad didn't know about it was Linn. If she'd spotted that (accidental) hug, I think she'd have gone ballistic, freaking out about her kid sister contaminating her best mate or something. She'd probably have made him burn all his clothes and wash himself in Dettol. As it was, I could tell by the way she'd acted normal (normally grumpy) at breakfast this morning that she'd seen nothing at all and that my secret (and Alfie's) was safe.

Actually, on the surface, *everything* seemed normal in our house this Friday morning. Colin was madly whirling around on the living-room rug, chasing his tail (OK, so that's not particularly normal for a *cat*, but who's quibbling). Winslet was under the kitchen table, chewing a shampoo bottle she'd nicked out of the bathroom (boy, was *she* in for a nasty surprise when her fangs bit through the plastic). Tor was drawing something with his crayons on the top of the kitchen table (on some paper, I mean, not on the table itself). Grandma was chatting politely to an electrician who'd come to fix the light problem that Dad hadn't managed to sort out last night (with a little help from Rolf, whose nose was currently in the guy's tool box, rooting around for spanners or gaffer tape or a stray ham sandwich, maybe).

But just because things *looked* normal on the surface, it didn't mean everything *was* normal. I mean, take Tor's drawing, for example. Was it of a boat? A car? A rocket? A kite? A duck-billed platypus? Nope, it wasn't a drawing of anything normal(ish) like that – it was of a ghost, whirling at the top of a room, unscrewing blobs ("Light bulbs!" Tor corrected me indignantly) from the ceiling.

The thing was, how could anything ever be normal in our house again, when there was a trick-playing spook in our midst? 'Cause despite what Linn and our neighbour Michael had said last night, it turned out there wasn't anything wrong with the fuses; Dad had sussed that much out when he'd hurried home from his night out. So what was this electrician going to do exactly? Wouldn't we have been better off getting a vicar or a psychic around to persuade our resident poltergeist to push off?

"Can I sleep with you again tonight, Ally?" Tor glanced up from his grim drawing.

"Nope, not tonight, Tor." I shook my head at him. "I've got everyone coming around for a sleepover in the garden."

I couldn't wait – all of us crammed into a six-man tent (with Billy crawling back to his own, solo tent when we finally got sleepy) – it would be a hoot. A laugh with the girls (and Billy); that was exactly what I needed to take my mind off all the spooksomeness going on around here...

"You're going to be sleeping *outside*?" Tor fixed his big Malteser-brown eyes on me.

"Yep," I nodded, thinking that I should ask Grandma for some money and go out to buy munchies for later.

"In the *dark*?" Tor gasped.

In the dark.

The dark.

Darkness.

Hmm ... why hadn't I thought of that before? Once we put the camp light and the torches off, there would be nothing between me and my friends and the darkness, except some flimsy tent material. Eeek! Maybe this wasn't such a fun idea after all...

"Ally! Can you get that, please?" Grandma shouted down from the first-floor landing.

"Sure," I nodded, glancing her way as I made a grab for the phone in the hall. How bizarre – all I could see of the electrician was his feet disappearing as he wriggled his way under the floorboards outside Tor's room. "Um, hello?"

"Hi, Ally..." mumbled a glum voice that sounded something like Billy.

"What's wrong with *you*?" I asked him. Normally

Billy sounded like Billy – cheerful, vague, annoying (especially annoying when he comes on the phone still eating his tea). I wasn't used to hearing him sound this gloomsville.

"So … did you have an interesting night last night after I left?"

Why was Billy asking that? Had he or one of the others spotted me and Alfie's (accidental) hug in the cupboard *after* all and told him about *that*?

Urgh…

"'Cause *I* certainly did," Billy continued, before I got a chance to come up with an answer.

"Oh, yeah? Why was it so interesting?" I asked, feeling relief flood through my veins. I know I said before that Billy and I don't keep secrets from each other, but … I lied. I certainly have *never* told him about fancying Alfie – I'd never hear the end of the teasing.

"I got arrested," Billy mumbled.

"You *what*?!"

"Well, OK, not *arrested* exactly – just cautioned."

"Billy, what are you on about?" I demanded. "You were here! You went home! How could you have got arrested, or cautioned or whatever?!"

"See, after I left you last night? Well, I phoned Steve, to tell him about what had happened at your house and everything. But anyway, Hassan was with him, and they were bored, and it still was pretty early and stuff, so I said I'd meet them and…"

Uh-oh – I think I could guess what was coming next.

"…and we thought it would be a laugh to go and do the gnome stuff again."

"Oh, Billy," I groaned.

"We were just doing this brilliant thing where we were putting an old pair of Hassan's pants on this gnome when this police car came out of nowhere! They took us down to the police station and kept us there for *hours*!"

"Oh, Billy," I groaned again, lost for words.

"Y'know, I'm *sure* someone in one of those posh houses must have called the police on us…"

Well, *duh* – there were three boys in that person's garden acting suspiciously with a pair of pants, so I guess they *would* have called the police. But I guessed that Billy didn't need me to point that out – not when several policemen would have done that already. And – omigod! – Billy's parents…!

"Billy – your mum and dad! What did *they* say?"

Billy's dad's all right, I *think*. He just never bothers talking very much; he's got his head permanently stuck in a newspaper every time I'm round there. But Billy's mum – ooh, she's a snob and a half and I couldn't see her being exactly thrilled about her son being picked up by the police.

"Um, well, *that's* what I was phoning about, Al."

"Go on, tell her!" snapped a shrewish voice in the background. Ah, so *that's* why Billy was sounding so different – his mother was hovering around him.

"It's just that I'm sort of grounded ... for ever."

"Don't make stupid jokes, Billy! Here, let *me* talk to her! Ally?"

"Hello, Mrs Stevenson," I said warily, hoping she didn't think *I* had anything to do with Billy's gnome escapades.

"Hello, Ally. Well, as you'll have heard, Billy has been a very stupid boy. More stupid than usual, I mean," she muttered tetchily. "So his father and I had no alternative but to ground him for a month, as punishment. That means he won't be coming to your sleepover tonight."

"Oh, OK," I answered her, only half-concentrating on what she was saying, thanks to a bit of a kerfuffle going on up on the first-floor landing.

"I'm sure a sensible girl like you understands the severity of what Billy has done," Mrs Stevenson wittered on.

What was the electrician holding exactly, now

he'd wriggled out from under the floorboards? And why was Grandma calling for Tor?

"Sorry, Mrs Stevenson – but my gran's calling me. I better go," I lied, keen to get away from Billy's mum's moaning (tell Billy! Not me!) and see what was going on upstairs.

As soon as I put the phone down, I followed Tor, who'd just scooted past me up the stairs.

"Tarzan!" Tor squealed at the madly scrabbling thing that the electrician was holding by the base of its tail.

"This rat belong to you, then, son?"

"'Snot a rat! It's a gerbil!" Tor said in a hurt voice, reaching over to take the dust-covered animal gently out of the man's hand.

"Well, that rat or gerbil or whatever you call it – that's the culprit!" the electrician announced, nodding towards Tarzan. "Gnawed straight through the light circuit cables! Wonder it wasn't electrocuted!"

"Tor, didn't you notice that Tarzan wasn't in his cage?" Grandma frowned at Tor over the top of her gold-rimmed specs.

"No," Tor shook his head, before sprinting off to his room to do a gerbil head-count and examine the cage for break-outs.

"You been bothered by any scratching noises

lately, have you?" the electrician asked Grandma, as he brushed the dust off his trousers.

"Yes!" I burst in. "*And* tapping!"

"That's your gerbily thing!" he shrugged. "That's the noise of it scurrying behind the skirting boards."

"See, Ally?" Grandma beamed at me all of a sudden. "I *told* you before that there would be a rational explanation for everything that's been going on around here!"

For one blissful second, I believed my gran. Then I remembered the painting that was turned upside down; the beans that were pointing south too; Rowan's keys in the freezer; Winslet in the kitchen-roll ghost outfit; the milk going green; the love spell pinned to the kitchen noticeboard.

Was a small hairy rodent really responsible for all that?

Yes, absolutely.

Well, that's the answer I *wished* I could believe...

Chapter 16

THE (NOT SO) GREAT OUTDOOR SLEEPOVER

"…and then Tor came running out of his room and said that Tarzan must have bent the bars open and escaped!"

"But hold on, Al," Kellie frowned at me, hugging her navy-blue sleeping bag close to her chest. "If Tarzan got out, why didn't the other gerbils sneak out too?"

"Beano and Dandy are too fat, apparently," I explained. "Tor said they'd have had to go on diets to sneak through the bars."

"But wait a minute," said Jen, stretching out on the top of her sleeping bag. "Isn't Tor mental about all his animals? How come he never noticed that Tarzan had escaped?"

"He's been a bit distracted since Stanley the goldfish died," I shrugged.

"Hold on, hold *on*! Why is everyone wittering on about fat gerbils and dead goldfish?" Kyra frowned at us all. "I thought this was supposed to be fun! I thought this was supposed to be a fun sleepover!"

And *I* thought this was supposed to be *my* fun sleepover, but since Kyra's parents had dropped her and her bag off earlier, she'd totally taken over. Kyra had raided the fridge and sorted out the snacks; Kyra had decided where we should pitch Chloe's giant tent; Kyra had decided whose sleeping bag should go next to whose; and now Kyra was even going to tell us what we should be talking about. I mean, good grief – don't you just yak away about anything and everything at a sleepover?

"So if you're not interested in talking about pets," Chloe asked Kyra pointedly, as Winslet lifted her hairy head in the corner and growled at nothing in particular, "what *do* you want to talk about, Kyra?"

Kyra gathered her long, skinny legs under her and widened her eyes at us all.

"Ghost stories! *That's* what you do on a night like this! You tell *ghost* stories!"

I saw Sandie give me an "uh-oh" look, but what could I do? Kyra had hijacked this sleepover and I didn't know how to stop her. For a second I wondered if Sandie was thinking what I was thinking; i.e. wishing that Billy *had* been here. He's just as loud and annoying as Kyra – in a totally *different* way – but maybe he'd have got us all doing funny stuff like listing our Top Ten ways to torture teachers ("Everyone in class pretends to have a sneezing attack! That *really* winds them up!"). But I was only fooling myself on two counts; 1) Sandie found Billy really irritating (and vice versa), and 2) Billy would probably think that the ghost story idea was *excellent*.

"Yeah? And I guess you happen to have a good ghost story, do you?" Salma smirked at Kyra, as she helped herself to another fun-size Snickers bar from the mound of food in the middle of the tent. (Rolf had been relegated to the house after he ate three Milky Ways – in their wrappers – and half a tub of sour cream and chive Pringles when we'd first come out here.)

"Course I do!" Kyra smirked back. "Are you ready? Is everyone sitting comfortably?"

As soon as she said that, I noticed Sandie, Kellie and Jen sink deeper into their sleeping bags.

"Get on with it!" Chloe teased Kyra, pinging a Wotsit at her head. "And this *better* be scary!"

"Oh, it is!" beamed Kyra, picking the Wotsit out of her curly ponytail and holding it out towards Winslet's waiting jaws. "Because it's a true story!"

"Oh, yeah?" Salma widened her eyes at Kyra. "And how do you know that?"

"I just do," said Kyra, in a low husky voice, as she

turned down the camping light slightly, casting weird shadows over the tent wall. "Now does everyone promise to shut up while I tell this?"

Everyone grunted and squeaked "Yes", depending on how reluctant/excited they were to hear Kyra's ghost story.

"OK," Kyra began, once she'd got silence. "There was this teenage couple in America, right, and they lived in this tiny town, miles from anywhere. So, anyway, this one weekend, they drove to the next town, where there was this disco or something happening."

"Whereabouts in America was this?" Kellie frowned.

"It doesn't matter!" Jen tried to shush her.

"But America's a big place! I just wanted to know! 'Cause my Auntie Vivette lives in Chicago and—"

"It *wasn't* near Chicago," Kyra butted in, trying to get everyone's attention back. "It was just some place in the country, OK?"

Kellie shrugged and slunk back into her sleeping bag.

"Anyhow," said Kyra, picking up where she left off. "After the disco or whatever, this couple starts driving home, only there's this huge storm, and the main road to their town is blocked off."

"By what?" Jen piped up. "A tree or something?"

"I don't know by what!" Kyra answered irritably. "That's not important!"

"OK..." Jen replied in a tiny, chastened voice.

"So the road was blocked, by *something*, and they had to take a side road, through these *daaaaaarrkkkk wooooodddsss...*"

If I hadn't been so scared I might have got the giggles at the stupid voice Kyra was now putting on.

"...and then – *blam!* – their car breaks down in the middle of nowhere, and they don't know what to do!"

"Couldn't they have phoned for help?" Salma suggested.

"This happened ages ago – *before* mobiles," Kyra replied through gritted teeth.

"Oh," mumbled Salma.

"So they've broken down, right?" Kyra continued. "And the guy says to the girl, 'You stay here – I'll walk back up to the main road and get help.' And so he goes, and the girl waits for ages and ages and ages, and then – *thump!* – something bangs on the roof of the car!"

I glanced around quickly at my friends and saw that Sandie had practically disappeared inside her sleeping bag.

"And then she hears it again!" Kyra went on,

wild-eyed and acting out the thump-thump with her hand on the groundsheet. "*Thump-thump-thump!* And she doesn't know what it could be, but—"

"—but," Salma interrupts, lazily helping herself to more nibbles, "it turns out to be the head of her boyfriend that some maniac in the woods has cut off."

Kyra pursed her lips and stared blackly at Salma for ruining her scary story.

"What?" Salma shrugged. "I heard that *years* ago when I was little! My big sister told it to me when we shared a room!"

OK, so Kyra's true story might not have been so true (it was just one of those freaky yarns that people like to pass around), but it had still cast a certain black mood over everyone in the tent, that funny stories about gerbils certainly hadn't.

"I need to go for a wee," said Jen, peeking out tortoise-style from her sleeping bag.

"So do I," Kellie chipped in.

"But I'm scared," said Jen.

"So am I," mumbled Kellie.

"Look, Dad left the lights on," I tried to point out, holding aside the tent flap so the girls could see the bright lights blazing in the kitchen and in the rest of the house.

"I will if *you* will!" Jen dared Kellie, and in two seconds flat both the girls were running squealing towards the back door. And two seconds after that, they'd started screaming for real and were hurtling themselves head-first back into the tent.

"What?! What happened?" I asked, panic-stricken.

"A ... a ... ghost!" Kellie's teeth chattered.

"On the w-w-wall!" Jen shivered beside her.

It was my garden, and scared or not, I was determined to peek out into it before Kyra beat me to that too.

For a spine-tingling, belly-flipping second – as I felt a cold night chill slap at my cheeks – I thought I saw the same, shimmering pale ghost as Jen and Kellie on the garden wall. And then common sense seeped into my brain and I realized that the white outline on the wall was none other than—

"It's only Tabitha!" I laughed, flopping back into the warmth of the sleeping-bag-filled tent.

"Who's Tabitha?" asked Jen, widening her tiny dark eyes so they looked almost real-sized instead of doll-sized for once.

"She's next door's cat! An old white Persian!" I smiled, as I described Michael and Harry's prized pet.

"Hey, girls!"

I jumped just as much as everyone else did at the sound of the deep male voice. Which was ridiculous really, considering that voice – and the smiling, dark-stubbled face that was now peering in the tent flap – was as familiar and lovely to me as my own dad. Because it *was* my own dad…

"Sorry! Didn't mean to scare anyone!" he apologized. "It's just that I heard screaming and I thought I'd better check on you all."

"We're OK, Dad!" I pulled myself together enough to answer him.

"Good, good. It's just that it is pretty late, and I thought maybe you girls could keep it down a little, so the neighbours didn't hear you or worry or anything."

None of us said anything; I think we were all trying to let our heart-rates settle back down to normal.

"It's just that I thought," Dad continued, as Winslet tried to lick his face, "that maybe you could all carry on with this camping thing … only maybe *indoors*."

I think Dad was nearly crushed into the lawn as me and my friends stampeded to the safety of the house with our sleeping bags trailing behind us…

Chapter 17

KYRA'S (SCARY) DARE

We were all up frighteningly early for people who'd gone to sleep frighteningly late.

Maybe me and the girls would have slept on (even though there was so little room on my bedroom floor that everyone was getting feet kicked in their faces), but Tor charged in with the dogs at half-past eight, demanding to know if I thought we should get Michael the vet to give Tarzan a checkup after his trauma.

("Er, no," was the answer to that, considering that when I last noseyed at our runaway gerbil, he seemed to have gained a very healthy appetite, from the way he was wolfing down Beano and Dandy's grub as well as his own. Ravenous he might have been, but he definitely wasn't poorly.)

After I'd shooed my little brother and our inquisitive dogs out of the room (Winslet had her eye on Jen's pink, spangly hairbrush, and Rolf's nose was working overtime trying to root out any leftover Pringle crumbs), my friends all started yawning and groaning themselves awake, and by half-nine, they'd finished their cornflakes, rolled up their sleeping bags and were squashing themselves and the big tent into Chloe's mum's car.

That's everyone except Kyra, of course – my weekend sleepover buddy.

"Listen," she'd yawned in my face as soon as we'd waved our mates away. "I think I'll go back to bed for a bit…"

Ha! Kyra might have hijacked last night's events (with fairly disastrous results), but that *wasn't* going to happen today. There was a certain ritual that happened every Saturday morning, and like it or not, Kyra was going to have to take part…

"Look!" Tor beamed, holding up a small, round thing covered in string.

"Cute!" I nodded, without really looking at it, and carried on piling pet supplies on the counter.

"See? Kyra? See?"

"Yeah, I see, Tor," Kyra faked a smile, while surreptitiously revealing her irritation by tapping her nails on the counter.

Tor darted happily over to where he'd picked up the string thing, and after putting it back, he started lifting up a black fluffy spider on elastic.

"Ally, *please*!" Kyra hissed at me, when she spotted what he was doing. "If I have to pretend to be interested in *one* more cat toy, I'll scream!"

Poor Kyra (and I don't say *that* very often) – Tor was so excited at the novelty of having her come along on our regular Saturday morning stock-up at the pet store that he was giving her the guided tour of every single item in the shop. Which Kyra was finding as riveting as a maths exam.

"Tor! Here! Grab a bag!" I tried to distract him into doing something useful, by passing him a plastic bag full of straw. Straw for hamsters/gerbils/mice to sleep in, that is – not for donkeys or horses to eat. Though having his own donkey is third on Tor's wish-list, right after 1) having his own pet dolphin and 2) owning a small-eared elephant shrew. (Don't ask.)

"Can we leave now before he shows me the entire range of budgie seed?" Kyra whispered desperately.

"Sure," I grinned, taking my change from the guy behind the counter. "Come on, we'll go for a hot chocolate now. Tor – lead the way!"

Two minutes later we were sitting in the window seat of Shufda's café, a couple of doors along from the pet store, gawping at people wandering by, as our mugs steamed in front of us.

Tor was absorbed in the animal magazine he'd just bought and Kyra and I were comfortably silent, both too tired after last night's sleepover to make any sensible (or non-sensible) conversation.

Me and all the girls, we'd ended up yakking deep into the night, fighting to tell funny stories and endless jokes. It was like we'd needed an antidote to Kyra's ghost story and the panic over the non-existent phantom on the garden wall. The fooling around had worked; instead of being spooked out, we'd all got the giggles so badly in the end that Linn came through and told us to shut up. Which just made us giggle *more* – as soon as we heard her bedroom door close, of course.

Sitting in silence, tired and daydreamy … it was pretty relaxing and nice. Till Kyra sparked into life and said something *really* worrying.

"You know something?" she announced, slapping her hand on the table and making me and Tor jump. "I've had an excellent idea for what we can do tonight!"

"Um, aren't we just watching a video round at Sandie's?" I reminded her of a vague plan we'd had to catch up on an old Jim Carrey movie the three of us had missed.

"Too boring!" Kyra snapped back, her eyes sparkling wickedly.

"So what's your idea?"

"It's— Oh, hold on."

Kyra broke off and rifled in her jean pocket for a second. Taking out a handful of pound coins, she grabbed one of Tor's hands and dropped the coins into it. Tor blinked at her blankly.

"Why don't you go and buy that string ... *thing* for the cats? As a present from me?"

Tor smiled in delight at Kyra, then turned to me to check that was all right.

"Go on, then!" I shrugged, but Tor was already racing out the door and back to the pet store before I got to the end of that very short sentence.

"That was nice of you." I frowned at Kyra, trying to guess at why she'd come over so generous all of a sudden.

"Well, I didn't want him to hear my plan. I don't want to corrupt his young mind!" Kyra grinned at me.

Gulp. What was she on about?

"See, last night, we were all a bunch of wimps, scaring ourselves over nothing, right?"

"Right," I nodded. We'd all giggled with embarrassment over breakfast this morning when we talked about how spooked we'd been.

"But *I* think we should do something *properly* scary tonight!"

"Like?" I heard myself squeak.

"Like hang out in Queen's Woods. Till it gets dark!"

Queen's Woods – they're even spooky in the daytime, even though they're very pretty and, er, foresty and everything. Where Highgate Woods nearby makes you think of squirrels and kicking leaves and taking dogs for walks, Queen's Woods is all gothic and dark, with a weird old Hansel and Gretel house by one exit and tonnes of old ivy-covered Victorian iron railings that fence in nothing in particular, which you can see below the tangles of dark fern and prickly bramble. If any film directors were scouting round north London for a location for a horror movie, Queen's Woods would be frighteningly perfect.

"So what do you think?" Kyra stared hard at me.

"I think I'd rather watch the Jim Carrey movie round at Sandie's," I told her straight.

"Oh, yeah?" Kyra narrowed her eyes at me. "Wait here – I'm going to go check Tor's got enough money for what he wants."

And with that, Kyra darted out of the café, leaving me totally confused, and with only three mugs of hot chocolate for company. Since when had Kyra turned into Tor's guardian angel? Since when was she so interested in checking his selection of cat toys? And since when had she ever given up on getting her way so easily?

I was still wondering and waiting a few minutes later when Tor came back into the caff with a contented smile on his face and a paper bag bulging with something round and presumably stringy.

"Where's Kyra?" I quizzed him, noticing a distinct lack of tall, skinny, pretty, mixed-race girl with him. (Did I miss out "annoying" from that list? Oops – silly me.)

"She's out there," Tor tilted his head towards the plate-glass window. "She's on the phone."

"Who's she calling?" I asked, while leaning side-ways and pressing my cheek against the window for a better look. Sure enough, loitering on the pavement further along the road was Kyra, smiling and twirling her fingers in the curls of her ponytail as she talked. And then she spotted me and gave me a cheery wave. Make that a *cheeky* wave.

"Kellie," Tor replied, examining his new cat toy at close quarters. "I heard her say."

"Kellie? Why's she calling Kellie? We only saw her an hour ago!"

As soon as I said that out loud, the truth sank in. Kyra had sneaked outside to call all our mates and try to persuade them that hanging out in Queen's Woods tonight was a sane idea. Well, *she'd* be lucky. None of them were going to be any keener than me to hang out in a seriously spooky wood after dark.

Er, wrong…

"Tor – here's some more money. Go and ask the nice man for a Coke or something."

"Cool!" Tor grinned, taking the money from her and darting over to the counter. (I think at this rate, by brother would probably be hoping that Kyra moved in with us for ever.)

"Listen, Ally, I've just rung around everyone and they're all up for Queen's Woods," Kyra said smugly, as she slithered back into her seat. "So you've *got* to do it now, too!"

"How did you get them to say yes?" I asked her, ignoring the last part of what she'd just said.

"I dared them," Kyra shrugged, before taking a noisy slurp from her mug.

"Sandie said yes to a *dare*?" I said incredulously. Sandie's super-shy. She'll often go along with stuff just 'cause she's too shy to argue her point, but one thing that would never work with Sandie – or any other shy person – is a dare. They're just not brave (make that *stupid*) enough to be suckered by that.

"No – everyone else went for the dare," Kyra corrected herself. "Sandie's doing it 'cause I said everyone else was. Including you."

"But I'm not!" I protested.

"What – *you're* going to sit at home while we're all out together?" Kyra laughed. "I don't *think* so!"

"But—"

"Shh – Tor's coming back over. We can't talk about this in front of him."

Good grief, Kyra had done it again, hijacking another night out. And I hadn't a clue how to get out of it...

Chapter 18

IF YOU GO DOWN TO THE WOODS TONIGHT...

"My bum's getting cold sitting on this stone."

"Sit on your jacket, then," Kyra told Salma.

"Couldn't we just walk around for—"

"No, Sal!" Kyra interrupted. "We agreed we'd sit here till the sun went down."

"Like in a mystic circle..." Jen chipped in, remembering Kyra's words as we walked here.

And where exactly *was* "here"? Right in the middle of Queen's Woods, that's where. In a dip; a little valley surrounded by wall-to-wall trees. Weirdly, this was the spot where someone, sometime (in the 1950s, or 60s, Dad thinks, but isn't really sure) decided to build a paddling pool, and what looks like a small shop – the sort that would sell you ice-cream and fizzy drinks on hot days.

Course the shop's all boarded up now, and the paddling pool is empty, except for a murky puddle of rainwater. It seems a bit sad when you look at it now, but if you think about it, putting a paddling pool and an ice-cream booth in the middle of a spooky Victorian wood is a pretty insane idea in the first place. It's about as smart as building a kids' sandpit in the middle of the North Circular ring road.

And as for wanting ice-cream or fizzy drinks on hot days, or stripping down to your swimmie for a cooling dip in the paddling pool, well, I'm sorry, but that was *never* going to happen – mainly because the trees are so tall and packed together in these woods that there's no *way* the sun could filter down as far as the pine needle-covered ground. In fact, I don't believe Queen's Woods ever, *ever* gets warm, even on the hottest summer day. There's always an icy chill in the air...

"I'm freezing!" Sandie moaned, budging up a little closer to me on the edge of the disused paddling pool where we were sitting.

"You should have worn more than just your T-shirt, then!" Chloe told her off. "You knew we were going to be here after dark!"

"Here," said Billy, getting up from the other side of the paddling pool, pulling off the grey hooded top he had tied around his waist, and holding it out towards Sandie.

That was sweet. A bit like when Sandie tried to thump him on the back when he was choking on his worm-flavoured drink the other day. You know, I know the two of them don't really click, but when they make little efforts like that to get on, it really makes my day.

"Thank you," Sandie murmured, taking the top from Billy and shivering her way into it.

"No problem. Just don't sweat on it," Billy spoiled the moment with a typically tasteless, tactless comment.

Sandie glowered at him as she struggled to zip up the front.

"And don't break the zip," Billy grinned.

"Do you want this back or something?" Sandie (amazingly!) said in a snippy tone, making like she was going to take the top off and give it back to him.

"No!" Billy protested, suddenly looking hurt.

What's he like? He just opens his trap and says stupid stuff and then wonders why people take offence...

"Y'know, if my mum knew we were all here on our own she'd go *mental*..." Kellie mumbled.

"Well, that's why you told her you were going to be round Sandie's tonight, isn't it?"

"Sandie's?" Kellie frowned at Kyra through the gloom. "I thought we were supposed to be round at Chloe's?"

"Kel, it doesn't matter *whose* place you told her

you'd be at," said Chloe, whose house we were definitely *not* in. "The point is, it's just a cover, right?"

Urgh – that was one of the parts of tonight that I *really* hated (apart from *being* here in the first place, of course) – fibbing to Dad. We'd all lied to all our parents, telling them that we were at Sandie's or Chloe's or anywhere that wasn't Queen's Woods in the dark.

"Hey, it's kind of dark, now, isn't it?" Jen suddenly suggested hopefully.

There was more to that sentence than met the eye, I knew. What Jen was *actually* saying was, "Hey, it's kind of dark, now, isn't it? So that's the dare done, isn't it? Now can we go home?"

"It's only just getting *properly* dark," Kyra answered her, staring up at the tops of the trees at the last of the dusk as the sky deepened from orange-streaked mid-blue into star-dotted navy blue.

"OK," I saw the outline of Billy shrug, as he pressed a button on his watch and lit up his face in a small pool of green neon. "So in a couple of minutes, it'll be properly dark. *Then* what do we do?"

"What's your hurry?" Kyra teased him, nodding at his watch. "Got to be somewhere?"

The somewhere Billy should have been, you might be thinking, was within the four walls of his house (like he should be every day for the next month). But his parents' plan to ground him had a fatal flaw in it; if they wanted to make sure he stayed home, they were going to have to ground themselves too. But only one night into his punishment, they'd swanned off to some play thing in the West End, leaving Billy home alone. Or not, as the case may be.

"You're doing *what*?" he'd garbled excitedly when we'd spoken on the phone earlier.

And so half an hour after his mum and dad had ambled off, Billy was locking up the house and running to meet all us girls at the Wood Vale entrance to Queen's Woods.

"I have to be home before my parents get back, remember?" Billy informed Kyra. "So whatever we're going to do, can we just get on with it?"

"Fine! Let's do it!" Kyra stood up and flicked her torch on.

"Er, what?" I asked, standing up and flicking my own torch on, even though I hadn't a clue what was coming next.

"We walk *that* way," said Kyra, pointing the beam of her torch in the opposite direction to the entrance we came in by, "right up to the Hansel and Gretel house. Then we go up on the veranda of it and look in through the window."

"Then?" I checked with her, gulping at the idea of peering in that spooky old house. It had sat empty and derelict for years, and even though part of it had been done up as a hippy café or something now, it was still a hundred per cent spooky.

"And then we can go home," said Kyra matter-of-factly, as if creeping up to deserted old houses in the middle of the night was as simple and straightforward as shopping for bananas in Sainsbury's.

"Go on, then!" I heard Chloe's voice, as she clicked on her torch, same as everyone else. "You go first, Kyra!"

And so our nervously giggling band of explorers set off up the path, bunched together for comfort.

"Stop!" gasped Salma, as we all clattered into her, beams of torchlight weaving wildly. "What's that light? Up there!"

"It's car headlights, you numpty!" Chloe sniggered, as the roar of an engine growled through the silence. "There's a road up there, remember?"

We gathered ourselves together, and started off again, this time splitting into a single-file crocodile as the path got narrower and plants and vines began to reach out and brush at our ankles.

"You won't let go, will you?" Sandie whispered behind me, wrapping her fingers around mine. "Promise?"

"Promise!" I whispered back.

"Stop!"

At Kyra's hissed instructions, we all froze, only just managing to avoid clattering into each other again.

"What?" said a voice that I thought was Kellie's.

"Listen!" Kyra urged.

We held our breath and listened.

The noise: it was a rustle, which then stopped.

Then rustled again, this time closer.

Then rustled fast, like some*thing* was running towards us...

Later, when my brain had snapped out of shock, I knew that the Thing was probably a fox or a rabbit or a squirrel or a rat, or anyway something that wasn't in the least bit supernatural. And the poor little fox/rabbit/squirrel/rat/whatever was most probably running *away* from us, not *towards* us. (I mean, if you were a small something, wouldn't you run away very fast at the sound of seven noisy berks stomping through your backyard?)

But right then, as shock and fear wibbled through my veins instead of blood, I did what everyone else did – and turned and ran, really, *really* fast towards the faraway exit, our torch beams bobbing and weaving alarmingly as we ran.

And then, as I panted my way in the direction of the welcoming streetlight out on to Wood Vale, I realized I'd broken my promise; I'd let go of Sandie's hand.

Despite being so spooked I could hardly breathe, I slowed down and spun the light of my torch all around me.

"Sandie?" I yelled desperately, as I saw Kellie and Jen sprint by.

"S'all right! She's with me!" I heard Billy's voice call out somewhere behind me.

Then there they were ... caught in the beam. And I tell you, that was the *spookiest* sight I'd seen all night.

Was that really Billy and Sandie *hugging* each other as they ran...?

Chapter 19

PANTING, FAINTING AND BIG, BIG HUGS

Being in Queen's Woods; it had seemed like an eternity. But when we were walking to Sandie's house – after we'd said an uneasy goodbye to Chloe, Salma, Kellie and Jen – Billy had told us how long we were actually in there for.

"Six minutes."

"Never! It was *much* longer than that!" Kyra had argued as we'd trudged along Park Road.

"Uh-uh," Billy shook his head. "I checked my watch when I met up with you lot and I checked my watch when we came out of there."

When he came out of there with his arm around Sandie, I thought to myself, although his arm was safely back by his side by the time they'd caught up with the rest of us under the street lamp...

God, when was I going to get the chance to ask Sandie what happened? Not tonight; not now we were back at Sandie's with Billy and Kyra both in tow. But then maybe the hugging thing hadn't meant anything at all … maybe it was just like me and Alfie in the cupboard, all accidental and spur of the moment. The only difference was, I fancied Alfie like crazy and Billy and Sandie could only just tolerate one another. Couldn't they?

"*Ooof!*" Sandie's mum winced.

"Mum?" said Sandie in a panic, gazing up at her mum.

"Don't worry! Just a bit of a twinge in my back – it's been coming and going. But you can't expect much more when you're carring all this weight around!" beamed Mrs Walker, doing this not-very-graceful vertical descent with a tray of drinks and biscuits on to the desk in Sandie's room, before patting her humongous bump.

"Are you sure?" Sandie blinked worriedly at her.

"Yes, petal, I'm sure. And us mummies know best!"

Urgh … why does Sandie's mother always insist on gabbing on in baby-talk?

"Um, thank you for the biscuits and everything, Mrs Walker!" I told her, being as polite as I could. (Even though she *said* she had, I don't think Sandie's mum has *ever* truly forgiven me for persuading Sandie to paint giant, mutant flowers on her bedroom wall.)

"Yeah, thank you, Mrs Walker!" Kyra smiled her

most charming I-didn't-try-and-lead-your-daughter-astray-tonight-honest-I-didn't smile.

"Thank you, Mrs Walker," Billy mumbled, blushing slightly and talking to the floor, 'cause of the fact that Sandie's mum's gigantic bump was about five centimetres away from his nose.

"So, weren't you having fun round at Kellie's?" Mrs Walker asked, as she straightened up and rubbed a hand over her very pregnant tummy.

Me, Sandie, Kyra and Billy all looked blankly at her (correction: Billy looked blankly at the *floor*), until I managed to scramble my brain into gear and remember that Kellie's was where Sandie had pretended she was going this evening.

"Um, Kellie wasn't feeling too well," I fibbed, feeling that old familiar twitch I always get at the corner of my mouth when I'm telling porky-pies.

"Oh, dear! Poor Kellie!" Mrs Walker sighed sympathetically, which made all of us feel ten times worse. "By the way, you don't all *have* to sit through here, you know; since Sandie's dad is away this weekend, you can always come and keep me company in the living room! *Casualty*'s just about to come on!"

"Er, no – you're all right, Mum," Sandie winced with embarrassment. "We're just going to listen to some CDs."

"Oh, super!" Mrs Walker twittered as she lumbered slowly towards the door. "Well, don't listen to your CDs for too long, sweetie! I know it's Saturday night, but I'm sure your friends all need their sleep as much as you do!"

See? That's more of the sort of toe-curlingly naff stuff that Sandie's mum comes out with all the time, like we should all still be watching *Bagpuss* and sleeping in Little Mermaid PJs. (Oh, except Sandie still does. Sleep in Little Mermaid PJs, I mean.)

"God, she's *so* mortifying!" Sandie cringed as soon as the door had shut.

"She's OK!" Billy stuck up for Mrs Walker, in a very gentlemanly fashion.

"Hey, she *has* left the room, Billy," I pointed out to him. "You *can* stop looking at the floor, you know."

Still blushing slightly, Billy lifted his head, and instantly cheered up when he saw the mound of biscuits Sandie's mum had set out for us.

"So when's your mum having her baby?" asked Kyra, biting into a Funny Face biscuit so hard that all the jam and cream oozed out of it.

I didn't know whether it was the idea of Sandie's mum giving birth combined with the oozy biscuit, but whatever it was, Billy started to flush and stared at the floor in obvious embarrassment again.

"Not for another few weeks," Sandie shrugged. "But you'd think it was tomorrow from the way my dad was faffing about yesterday. He's at this work conference thing in Yorkshire, but he was talking about it like it was happening on Mars, and that it would take him *months* to get back if Mum started, y'know, having the baby early or anything."

Now I couldn't see anything of Billy's face; he had his head hung so low that all I was looking at was the very top of his baseball cap, full on.

"Yeah? Your dad's away at a work thing?" Kyra nodded, crossing one long, skinny brown leg over the other. "So's mine. Only my mum's gone with him too—"

Billy's head shot up at the sound of the long, peculiar groaning sound coming from outside the room somewhere.

"Is it a ghost?" Sandie gasped, slapping her hands over her face.

"Er … I think it's your mum, Sand!" I answered, sure that the noise was pretty much human.

In one bound, all four of us were out in the hall, and there, on the floor in the living-room doorway – while sirens rang out on *Casualty* – was Mrs Walker, lying on her back, groaning and clutching her huge tummy.

"Omigod!" Sandie whimpered.

"Um, is … is … is the baby, um, *coming*, Mrs Walker?" I asked nervously, trying to remember any birth-related episodes of *ER* (much better than *Casualty*) that I'd seen on TV.

"*YES!!*" Mrs Walker barked in a tone of bark I'd never heard kindly-but-corny Mrs Walker use before.

"Omigod!" Sandie whimpered again.

"Omigod!" Kyra slapped her hand over her mouth.

Omigod! I thought loudly in my head.

"It's cool! Everything's going to be cool!" Billy suddenly announced. "Someone, er, get a pillow for her head! And someone else, get her some towels or a blanket to, er, put down *that* end! And I'll, er, call an ambulance!"

As Billy started hammering 999 into the phone, Sandie, Kyra and I stared at each other for a second, stunned at our own stupidity in the face of a crisis and totally bamboozled at Billy's impressive attempts to deal with the situation. You know, I think he only lasted in the Boy Scouts for two weeks (if I remember right he got chucked out for tying a knot into a rude shape), but in that short time, he must have got his Emergency Birth badge or something.

"I'll get the pillows and towels!" Sandie announced.

"Um, Mrs Walker! The operator says you've got to start counting how often the, um, contraction-y things are coming!" Billy shouted from the phone.

"QUICKLY!" Mrs Walker shouted back. "They're coming QUICKLY!"

"I'll grab that clock," Kyra announced, dashing for the mantelpiece. "It's got a second hand…"

"Um, OK, Mrs Walker, the operator says we should try and time them till the ambulance gets here!" Billy relayed the information to Sandie's prostrate mum. "But she says, can you start doing some breathing stuff you're supposed to be doing?"

At Billy's request, just as Sandie thrust a couple of pillows under her head, Mrs Walker started to do this pursed lipped panting that I've seen people on *ER* do when they're in labour.

Wow, Billy…

"Yeah, she's doing it," Billy said into the phone. "You're, um, doing great, Mrs Walker! The ambulance is on it's way! It's nearly here!"

"AAAARRRGGHHH!" Mrs Walker yelled, making us all jump.

"It's OK!" I tried to tell her, not knowing what else to say. ("Please can I go home? 'Cause this is scarier than being stuck in Queen's Woods!" wouldn't have been too helpful, even if it *was* the truth.)

However lame my remark was, it seemed to do the trick, as Mrs Walker reached out for my hand and started clutching it till it felt like she might break some bones.

"You're brilliant!" I heard Sandie say, somewhere above me, and when I looked around – through the red-misted pain of Mrs Walker crushing my hand – I saw that Sandie was saying it to Billy.

"No problem," I heard Billy answer. "Er, Sandie ... what's all that stuff on the floor?"

Sure enough, there in the hall was a huge puddle of cloudy liquid.

"Her waters have broken!" Kyra announced loudly, like an extra on a medical show. I guess, same as me, she'd heard the term used before about people having babies, but just never seen it.

Billy had been admirably brave up till that point, but *something* about that puddle having *something* to do with Sandie's mum's bump seemed to tip him over the edge.

"Billy!" Sandie shrieked as he fainted away, still holding on to the phone. "Billy, *please* ... oh, *please* ... wake up, Billy, *please* ... oh, *please*!"

This whole night was getting more and more bizarre by the *milli*second. Kyra stared at me, gobsmacked, over the top of Mrs Walker's bump, just as stunned as I was to see Sandie clutch Billy's head in her lap, interspersing every one of her "please"s with a kiss to Billy's forehead.

I'm sorry, but could this night *get* any weirder…?

Chapter 20

WOW TIMES TEN

It was Sunday night: Sandie's little sister was nearly one day old.

"Is she cute?" I asked her down the phone.

"Yes," Sandie answered in a hesitant voice. "Cute in a pickled, pruney way..."

Fair enough. I think all babies are meant to come out looking pickled and pruney, aren't they? I was just glad that me, Kyra, Billy and Sandie didn't have to witness the actual moment when pruney Miss Walker junior made her way into the world – the super-speedy ambulance arrived just in time and whisked Mrs Walker and her bump (and Sandie) off to the Whittington Hospital about two minutes after Billy blacked out.

He came around OK, by the way. He didn't need oxygen or smelling salts or anything else medical – just a few kisses on the forehead from Sandie seemed to do the trick.

Which brought me round to the question I had to ask...

"Er, Sandie?"

"Yes?"

"What exactly is the score with you and Billy...?"

"Uh, listen, I can't really speak..." she muttered.

Fair enough. Her dad – who'd scurried back from Yorkshire in the middle of the night – was probably hovering around.

"...'cause Billy's here."

Billy was at the *hospital*? What – were my best friends holding hands and cooing over Mrs Walker's new baby together? Was Billy being the hero again and running off to get coffees for Sandie and her dad and everyone? What the *flip* was going on?!

"OK, so you can't talk," I told her, vaguely aware of Rowan stampeding down the stairs beside me shrieking something about some knocking or something and then diving into the living room. "So just say yes or no. Are you and Billy, um, going *out* now?"

"Uh ... yes. I think so!" Sandie giggled.

Well, wow.

Wow times ten.

I couldn't think of anything to say to that bizarre piece of information, so instead I just said, "But what about Billy being grounded?"

It had been so ... not *right* this morning, when I trudged up to "our" bench with the dogs and Kyra and he wasn't there. (Kyra, incidentally, was up in my room at this precise moment, waiting patiently for me to come back and relay the gossip, while she blasted all my CDs at full volume.)

"His parents are really proud of him for helping out with my mum and everything," I could practically hear Sandie beam at me. "So they didn't mind him sneaking out last night or coming here this evening. Actually, they're here too, talking to my dad."

Good grief. I'd entered a parallel universe, where my two best friends fancied each other instead of ignoring each other, and hung out – with their parents – over the coffee machine at the local hospital. It was like what Rowan had said when I told her about it earlier: "There's a thin line between love and hate." It had sounded very smart and deep and profound, until she told me it was the lyric to an old song she couldn't remember the name of, *or* who'd done it. But Ro went on to say she'd seen it happen *loads* of times – people who take the trouble to dislike each other are often actually hiding the fact that they're really, really drawn to each other. Seemed as if that's what had gone on with Sandie and Billy all this time. Maybe that's where I'd gone wrong with Alfie ... maybe I should try to *hate* him or something.

You know, I think my brain might just self-combust at the oddness of it all.

"Look, I'd better go..." said Sandie, just as I realized I'd better too. Something severely strange was going on in my house, as I could tell from the fact that Dad was now bounding up the stairs with a worried-looking Rowan following him.

"The tapping – it's back, Ally!" she called to me over the bannister.

Uh-oh...

It was like Grandma said; everything spooky can be explained rationally.

The tapping that Rowan had heard at her first-floor window? It was a broken old cassette, being dangled from a length of unravelled brown tape from my bedroom window. Kyra had swung it back and forth till it had enough sway to tap-tap against the glass.

And there was more, we found out, as soon as Dad opened Rowan's window and sussed where the cassette was being dangled from.

"Mum's painting hanging upside down?" Rowan asked Kyra, as me, Linn, Ro, Dad and Kyra held a pow-wow around the kitchen table.

"Yep," admitted Kyra, her chin sinking further down into her hands. "I just thought it would be … well, *funny*. Just because you'd all been going on about ghosts and everything."

"The upside-down beans too?" I asked her.

She nodded.

Of course! Kyra had come round last week, and heard us rabbitting on about the scratch-scratching and the tap-tapping (which turned out to be Tarzan the runaway gerbil).

"And you put my keys in the freezer?" Ro checked with her.

Kyra nodded glumly.

"Wait a minute – did you dress Winslet up in all that kitchen roll?" I asked her, remembering the ghostly dog incident that had freaked Sandie out so much.

Kyra nodded again.

"It was just meant to be a joke!" she said lamely.

"The milk going green in our fridge – was that you too?" Linn narrowed her eyes at my "friend" (I use that term loosely).

"It was food colouring. I put some in when I came round that afternoon. It all sinks to the bottom of the plastic carton and then when someone moves it…"

Kyra didn't finish her explanation, but I could

just picture those green streaks whirling up from the bottom of the milk carton on Wednesday night.

"And did you stick that ... book thing on the kitchen noticeboard?" I asked her, remembering the torn Charming Charm pinned to the cork board on Thursday night, right before Tarzan chewed through the light circuit.

"Uh-huh," Kyra shrugged sorrowfully, aware that her excellent prank had got *way* out of hand.

"Well, Kyra," Dad frowned at her. "I've only got one thing to say…"

I saw Kyra gulp.

"…well done! You caught us all out!"

Kyra's face relaxed into a shy, surprised smile.

"Only, please – never do anything like that again! Deal?" Dad grinned, holding his hand out for her to shake.

"Deal!" Kyra giggled with relief.

"I'll get the kettle on," Linn sighed wearily at my dad's softness as she headed for the mugs and tea bags.

"*How* did the food dye thing work again?" Rowan quizzed Kyra, her curiosity blanking out the wibble-wobbles she'd had over the last week or so.

And me? Kyra's confession hadn't taken me too much by surprise. It wasn't like I'd expected such a straightforward answer to all the mental stuff that had been going on. The thing was, I was still reeling from the shock of the strangest thing of all.

I mean, who needs ghosts, poltergeists and spooky tap-tappings when your two best friends suddenly start *fancying* each other?

I tell you, that is *pretty* weird weirdness...

Ally ;c]

PS Linn didn't speak to Kyra for a whole week, she was so mad at her for "scarring Tor for life", as she put it. She finally quit that when she caught Tor telling Spartacus the tortoise that he must never be afraid of ghosts because they don't exist. Linn felt a whole lot more relieved after that, and same goes for Spartacus, I'm sure. (Ahem...)

PS (again) Tor might not have been scarred for life, but I think his little friend Amir has been. He's still Tor's best buddy at the summer school thing (Tor's teaching him to speak English, he says, but considering that Tor hardly ever *speaks*, that means Amir will probably only get a grasp of the language by the time he's forty-five). Anyway, he's flatly refused every invitation to come round our house again. At least while Rowan the resident weirdo lives here...

PS (again, again) Sandie's mum (Sandra) and dad (Robert) apparently spent months trawling through baby name books. And what did they end up calling Sandie's new sister? Roberta. What a waste of money those books were...

PPS Speaking of books, when all us girls got together this week, Kyra suggested that we try another of the love spells. Everyone overruled her and we watched Jim Carrey's new video instead. (Anyway, it would have been kind of hard to do another of those spells since I put the book in the bin last Monday.)

PPPS Sandie and Billy have been going out for one whole week now, and I *still* don't get it. Turns out they both "always kind of fancied each other". Huh – they managed to hide *that* well all this time. Good grief, I'll never get the hang of this love thing...

SIGN UP NOW!

For exclusive news, competitions and further information about Karen and her books, sign up to the Karen McCombie newsletter now!

Just email

publicity@scholastic.co.uk

And don't forget to check out her website –

www.karenmccombie.com

Karen says...

"It's sheeny and shiny, furry and er, funny in places! It's everything you could want from a website and a weeny bit more..."

Karen McCombie

"A funny and talented author"
Books Magazine

Once upon a time (OK, 1990), Karen McCombie jumped in her beat-up car with her boyfriend and a very bad-tempered cat, leaving her native Scotland behind for the bright lights of London and a desk at "J17" magazine. She's lived in London and acted like a teenager ever since.

The fiction bug bit after writing short stories for "Sugar" magazine. Next came a flurry of teen novels, and of course the best-selling "Ally's World" series, set around and named after Alexandra Palace in North London, close to where Karen lives with her husband Tom, little daughter Milly and an assortment of cats.

Funny FAQs

When I do talks at schools, book shops, libraries and festivals, I get asked lots of interesting, sensible questions about me, my life, and writing my books. And then I get the NSFAQs (Not So Frequently Asked Questions). Check out some below!

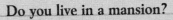

Do you live in a mansion?
Er, nope. Until a couple of years ago, we lived in a very nice two-bedroomed flat - then we moved round the corner to a three-bedroomed terraced house, which we added a loft room office to. We've got a swimming pool, though. (OK, it's a metre-wide blow-up paddling pool, decorated with freaky-looking dolphins that our daughter Milly loves!)

Are you Scottish?
Well, I have a very Scottish last name and a Scottish accent, so, I guess, yes - I AM pretty Scottish! But I've lived in London since 1990, so I consider myself very much British(ish).

What's your favourite football team?
Er, don't have one. If there's such a thing at football dyslexia, I think I may have it. When I try and watch a match on TV, all I see is a jumble of legs running and can't figure out who's who, or where they're headed.

What's your favourite colour?
Yellow to look at, green to wear. But I'm pretty addicted to looking at colours: from the pink of cherry blossoms to the peach of sunsets to the weird rainbow swirls of oil in a puddle...

To: You
From: Stella
Subject: Stuff

Hi,

You'd think it would be cool to live by the sea with all that sun,
sand and ice cream. But, believe me, it's not such a breeze.
I miss my best mate Frankie, my terror twin brothers drive me
nuts and my mum and dad have gone daft over the country
dump, sorry, "character cottage", that we're living in. I'm bored,
and I'm fed up with being the new girl on the block.
Hey! Maybe if we hang out together we could have some fun
here. Whadya think?
Catch up with me in the rest of the *Stella Etc.* series.
I bet we'll have loads to talk about.
CU soon.
LOL

stella
XXX

PS Here's a pic of me on a bad hair day (any day actually) with my
mate Frankie. I'm the one on the right!

"Super-sweet and cool as an ice cream" *Mizz*

aLLY'S WORLd

**Hi,
There's lots going on in my world – here's just some of what I have to deal with!!**

2 SiSteRS – 1 bOSSY,
1 bONKeRS
1 SPaCe-Cadet bROtheR
1 dad
O MUM
1 SCRUffY hOUSe iN a NiCe PLaCe
with a fUNNY NaMe
1 gReat View fROM MY bedROOM
2 dOgS – WiNSLet aNd ROLf
(dON't eVeN aSK)
5 CatS – 1'S CaLLed COLiN
Oh, aNd fRieNdS – LOtS.

Now that you've finished this story, get into one of my other adventures – there's heaps to choose from.

"Once you start reading you can't stop" *Mizz*